THE THREAD OF GOLD

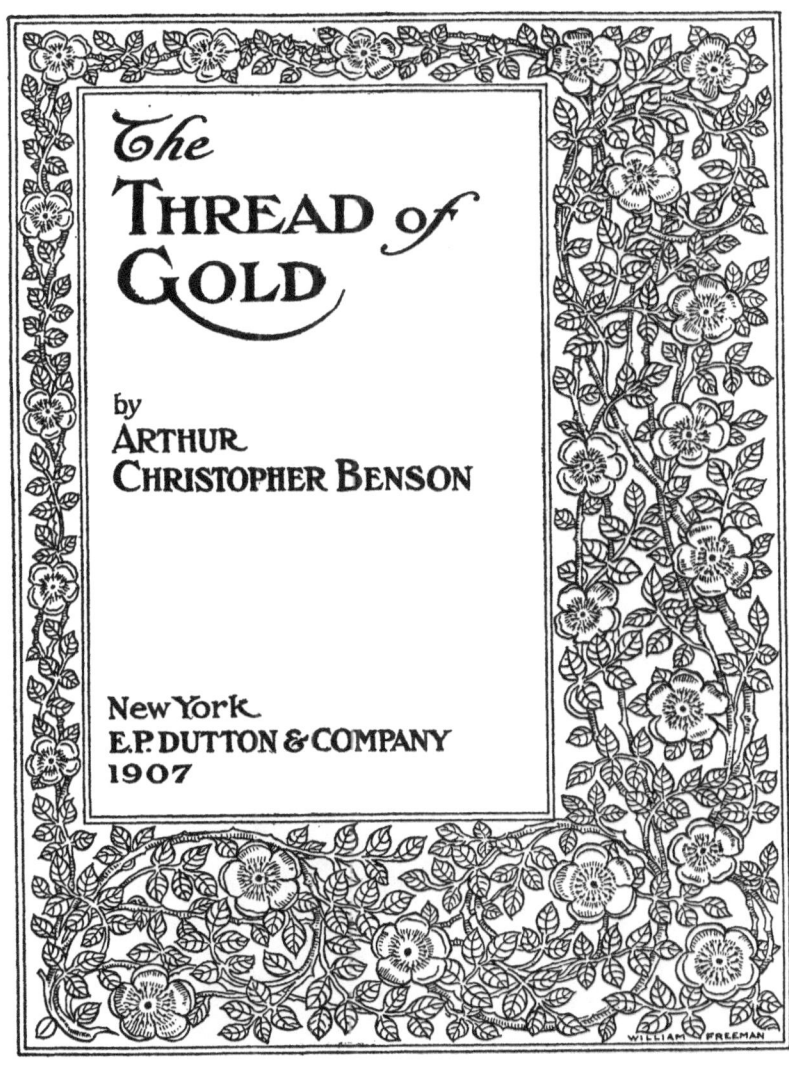

The
THREAD of
GOLD

by
ARTHUR
CHRISTOPHER BENSON

New York
E. P. DUTTON & COMPANY
1907

PREFACE.

I SATE to-day, in a pleasant hour, at a place called *The Seven Springs,* high up in a green valley of the *Cotswold* hills. Close beside the road, seven clear rills ripple out into a small pool, and the air is musical with the sound of running water. Above me, in a little thicket, a full-fed thrush sent out one long-drawn cadence after another, in the joy of his heart, while the lengthening shadows of bush and tree crept softly over the pale sward of the old pasture-lands, in the westering light of the calm afternoon.

These springs are the highest head-waters of the *Thames,* and that fact is stated in a somewhat stilted Latin hexameter carved on a stone of the wall beside the pool. The so-called *Thames-head* is in a meadow down below *Cirencester,* where a deliberate engine pumps up, from a hidden well, thousands of gallons a day of the purest water, which begins the service of man at once by helping to swell the scanty flow of the *Thames and Severn Canal.* But *The Seven Springs* are the highest hill-fount of Father *Thames* for all that, streaming as they do from the eastward ridge of the great oölite crest of the downs that overhang *Cheltenham.*

As soon as those rills are big enough to form a
stream, the gathering of waters is known as the
Churn, which, speeding down by *Rendcomb* with
its ancient oaks, and *Cerney,* in a green elbow of
the valley, join the *Thames* at *Cricklade.*

It was of the essence of poetry to feel that the
water-drops which thus babbled out at my feet in
the spring sunshine would be moving, how many
days hence, beside the green playing-fields at *Eton,*
scattered, diminished, travel-worn, polluted; but
still, under night and stars, through the sunny
river-reaches, through hamlet and city, by water-
meadow or wharf, the same and no other. And
half in fancy, half in earnest, I bound upon the
heedless waters a little message of love for the fields
and trees so dear to me.

What a strange parable it all made! the sparkling
drops so soon lost to sight and thought alike, each
with its own definite place in the limitless mind of
God, all numbered, none forgotten; each drop,
bright, new-born, and fresh as it appeared, racing
out so light-heartedly into the sun,—yet as old, and
older, than the rocks from which it sprang! How
often had those water-drops been woven into cloud-
wreaths, through what centuries they had leapt and
plunged among sea-billows, or lain cold and dark
in the ocean depths, since the day when this mass of
matter that we call the earth had been cut off and

sent whirling into space, a molten drop from the fierce vortex of its central sun! And, what is the strangest thought of all, I can sit here myself, a tiny atom spun from drift of storms, and concourse of frail dust, and, however dimly and faintly, depict the course of things, trace, through some subtle faculty, the movement of the mind of God through the æons; and yet, though I can send my mind into the past and the future, though I can see the things that are not and the things that are, I am denied the least inkling of what it all signifies, what the slow movement of the ages is all aimed at, and even what the swift interchange of light and darkness, pain and pleasure, sickness and health, love and hate, is meant to mean to me—whether there *is* a purpose and an end at all, or whether I am just allowed, for my short space of days, to sit, a bewildered spectator, at some vast and unintelligible drama.

Yet to-day the soft sunshine, the babbling springs, the valley brimmed with haze, the bird's sweet song, all seem framed to assure me that God means us well, urgently, intensely well. " My Gospel," wrote one to me the other day, whose feet move lightly on the threshold of life, " is the Gospel of contentment. I do not see the necessity of asking myself uneasy and metaphysical questions about the Why and the Wherefore and the What."

The necessity? Ah, no! But if one is forced, against one's will and hope, to go astray in the wilderness out of the way, to find oneself lonely and hungry, one must needs pluck the bitter berries of the place for such sustenance as one can. I doubt, indeed, whether one is able to compel oneself into and out of certain trains of thought. If one dislikes and dreads introspection, one will doubtless be happier for finding something definite to do instead. But even so, the thoughts buzz in one's ears; and then, too, the very wonder about such things in the world, such as *Hamlet,* or Keats's *Ode to the Nightingale,* things we could not well do without. Who is to decide which is the nobler, wiser, righter course—to lose oneself in a deep wonder, with an anxious hope that one may discern the light; or, on the other hand, to mingle with the world, to work, to plan, to strive, to talk, to do the conventional things? We choose (so we call it) the path that suits us best, though we disguise our motives in many ways, because we hardly dare to confess to ourselves how frail is our faculty of choice at all. But, to speak frankly, what we all do is to follow the path where we feel most at home, most natural; and the longer I live the more I feel that we do the things we are impelled to do, the works prepared for us to walk in, as the old collect says. How often, in real life, do we see any one

making a clean sweep of all his conditions and surroundings, to follow the path of the soul? How
often do we see a man abjure wealth, or resist am-
bition, or disregard temperament, *unexpectedly?*
Not once, I think, to speak for myself, in the whole
of my experience.

This, then, is the *motif* of the following book:
that, whether we are conquerors or conquered, triumphant or despairing, prosperous or pitiful, well
or ailing, we are all these things through Him that
loves us. We are here, I believe, to learn rather
than to teach, to endure rather than to act, to be
slain rather than to slay; we are tolerated in our
errors and our hardness, in our conceit and our security, by the great, kindly, smiling Heart that
bade us be. We can make things a little easier for
ourselves and each other; but the end is not there:
what we are meant to become is joyful, serene,
patient, waiting momently upon God; we are to
become, if we can, content not to be content, full
of tenderness and loving-kindness for all the frail
beings that, like ourselves, suffer and rejoice. But
though we are bound to ameliorate, to improve, to
lessen, so far as we can, the brutal promptings of
the animal self that cause the greatest part of our
unhappiness, we have yet to learn to hope that when
things seem at their worst they are perhaps at their
best, for then we are, indeed, at work upon our hard

lesson; and perhaps the day may come when, looking back upon the strange tangle of our lives, we may see that the time was most wasted when we were serene, easy, prosperous, and unthinking, and most profitable when we were anxious, overshadowed, and suffering. *The Thread of Gold* is the fibre of limitless hope that runs through our darkest dreams; and just as the water-drop which I saw break to-day from the darkness of the hill, and leap downwards in its channel, will see and feel, in its seaward course, many sweet and gentle things, as well as many hard and evil matters, so I, in a year of my pilgrimage, have set down in this book a frank picture of many little experiences and thoughts, both good and evil. Sometimes the water-drop glides in the sun among mossy ledges, or lingers by the edge of the copse, where the hazels lean together; but sometimes it is darkened and polluted, so that it would seem that the foul oozings that infect it could never be purged away. But the turbid elements, the scum, the mud, the slime—each of which, after all, has its place in the vast economy of things—float and sink to their destined abode; and the crystal drop, released and purified, runs joyfully onward in its appointed way.

A. C. B.

CIRENCESTER, *8th April,* 1907.

THE THREAD OF GOLD

INTRODUCTION

I HAVE for a great part of my life desired, perhaps more than I have desired anything else, to
make a beautiful book; and I have tried, perhaps
too hard and too often, to do this, without ever
quite succeeding; by that I mean that my little
books, when finished, were not worthy to be com-
pared with the hope that I had had of them. I
think now that I tried to do too many things in my
books, to amuse, to interest, to please persons who
might read them; and I fear, too, that in the back
of my mind there lay a thought, like a snake in its
hole—the desire to show others how fine I could be.
I tried honestly not to let this thought rule me;
whenever it put its head out, I drove it back; but of
course I ought to have waited till it came out, and
then killed it, if I had only known how to do that;
but I suppose I had a secret tenderness for the little creature as being indeed a part of myself.

But now I have hit upon a plan which I hope may succeed. I do not intend to try to be interesting and amusing, or even fine. I mean to put into my book only the things that appear to me deep and strange and beautiful; and I can happily say that things seem to me to be more and more beautiful every day. As when a man goes on a journey, and sees, in far-off lands, things that please him, things curious and rare, and buys them, not for himself or for his own delight, but for the delight of one that sits at home, whom he loves and thinks of, and wishes every day that he could see;— well, I will try to be like that. I will keep the thought of those whom I love best in my mind— and God has been very good in sending me many, both old and young, whom I love—and I will try to put down in the best words that I can find the things that delight me, not for my sake but for theirs. For one of the strangest things of all about beauty is, that it is often more clearly perceived when expressed by another, than when we see it for ourselves. The only difficulty that I see ahead is that many of the things that I love best and that give me the best joy, are things that cannot be told, cannot be translated into words: deep and gracious mysteries, rays of light, delicate sounds.

But I will keep out of my book all the things, so far as I can, which bring me mere trouble and

heaviness; cares and anxieties and bodily pains and
dreariness and unkind thoughts and anger, and all
uncleanness.   I cannot tell why our life should be
so sadly bound up with these matters; the only comfort is that even out of this dark and heavy soil
beautiful flowers sometimes spring. For instance,
the pressure of a care, an anxiety, a bodily pain, has
sometimes brought with it a perception which I
have lacked when I have been bold and joyful and
robust.   A fit of anger too, by clearing away
little clouds of mistrust and suspicion, has more
than once given me a friendship that endures and
blesses me.

But beauty, innocent beauty of thought, of
sound, of sight, seems to me to be perhaps the most
precious thing in the world, and to hold within it a
hope which stretches away even beyond the grave.
Out of silence and nothingness we arise; we have
our short space of sight and hearing; and then into
the silence we depart.   But in that interval we are
surrounded by much joy.   Sometimes the path is
hard and lonely, and we stumble in miry ways; but
sometimes our way is through fields and thickets,
and the valley is full of sunset light.   If we could
be more calm and quiet, less anxious about the impression we produce, more quick to welcome what
is glad and sweet, more simple, more contented,
what a gain would be there!   I wonder more and

more every day that I live that we do not value
better the thought of these calmer things, because
the least effort to reach them seems to pull down
about us a whole cluster of wholesome fruits,
grapes of Eschol, apples of Paradise. We are
kept back, it seems to me, by a kind of silly fear of
ridicule, from speaking more sincerely and in-
stantly of these delights.

I read the *Life* of a great artist the other day
who received a title of honour from the State. I
do not think he cared much for the title itself, but
he did care very much for the generous praise of his
friends that the little piece of honour called forth.
I will not quote his exact words, but he said in
effect that he wondered why friends should think it
necessary to wait for such an occasion to indulge in
the noble pleasure of praising, and why they should
not rather have a day in the year when they could
dare to write to the friends whom they admired and
loved, and praise them for being what they were.
Of course if such a custom were to become general,
it would be clumsily spoilt by foolish persons, as all
things are spoilt which become conventional. But
the fact remains that the sweet pleasure of praising,
of encouraging, of admiring and telling our admiration, is one that we English people are sparing
ing of, to our own loss and hurt. It is just as false
to refrain from saying a generous thing for fear

of being thought insincere and what is horribly called gushing, as it is to say a hard thing for the sake of being thought straightforward. If a hard thing must be said, let us say it with pain and tenderness, but faithfully. And if a pleasant thing can be said, let us say it with joy, and with no less faithfulness.

Now I must return to my earlier purpose, and say that I mean that this little book shall go about with me, and that I will write in it only strange and beautiful things. I have many businesses in the world, and take delight in many of them; but we cannot always be busy. So when I have seen or heard something that gives me joy, whether it be a new place, or, what is better still, an old familiar place transfigured by some happy accident of sun or moon into a mystery; or if I have been told of a generous and beautiful deed, or heard even a sad story that has some seed of hope within it; or if I have met a gracious and kindly person; or if I have read a noble book, or seen a rare picture or a curious flower; or if I have heard a delightful music; or if I have been visited by one of those joyful and tender thoughts that set my feet the right way, I will try to put it down, God prospering me. For thus I think that I shall be truly interpreting his loving care for the little souls of men. And I call my book *The Thread of Gold,* because this beauty

of which I have spoken seems to me a thing which
runs like a fine and precious clue through the dark
and sunless labyrinths of the world.

And, lastly, I pray God with all my heart, that
he may, in this matter, let me help and not hinder
his will. I often cannot divine what his will is, but
I have seen and heard enough to be sure that it is
high and holy, even when it seems to me hard to
discern, and harder still to follow. Nothing shall
here be set down that does not seem to me to be
perfectly pure and honest; nothing that is not wise
and true. It may be a vain hope that I nourish,
but I think that God has put it into my heart to
write this book, and I hope that he will allow me to
persevere. And yet indeed I know that I am not
fit for so holy a task, but perhaps he will give me
fitness, and cleanse my tongue with a coal from his
altar fire.

I

VERY deep in this enchanted land of green hills in which I live, lies a still and quiet valley. No road runs along it; but a stream with many curves and loops, deep-set in hazels and alders, moves brimming down. There is no house to be seen; nothing but pastures and little woods which clothe the hill-sides on either hand. In one of these fields, not far from the stream, lies a secluded spot that I visit duly from time to time. It is hard enough to find the place; and I have sometimes directed strangers to it, who have returned without discovering it. Some twenty yards away from the stream, with a ring of low alders growing round it, there is a pool; not like any other pool I know. The basin in which it lies is roughly circular, some ten feet across. I suppose it is four or five feet deep. From the centre of the pool rises an even gush of very pure water, with a certain hue of green, like a faintly-tinted gem. The water in its flow makes a perpetual dimpling on the surface; I have never known it to fail even in the longest droughts; and in sharp frosty days there hangs a little smoke above it, for the water is of a noticeable warmth.

This spring is strongly impregnated with iron, so strongly that it has a sharp and medical taste; from what secret bed of metal it comes I do not know, but it must be a bed of great extent, for, though the spring runs thus, day by day and year by year, feeding its waters with the bitter mineral over which it passes, it never loses its tinge; and the oldest tradition of the place is that it was even so centuries ago.

All the rest of the pool is full of strange billowy cloudlike growths, like cotton-wool or clotted honey, all reddened with the iron of the spring; for it rusts on thus coming to the air. But the orifice you can always see, and that is of a dark blueness; out of which the pure green water rises among the vaporous and filmy folds, runs away briskly out of the pool in a little channel among alders, all stained with the same orange tints, and falls into the greater stream at a loop, tinging its waters for a mile.

It is said to have strange health-giving qualities; and the water is drunk beneath the moon by old country folk for wasting and weakening complaints. Its strength and potency have no enmity to animal life, for the water-voles burrow in the banks and plunge with a splash in the stream; but it seems that no vegetable thing can grow within

it, for the pool and channel are always free of
weeds.

I like to stand upon the bank and watch the green
water rise and dimple to the top of the pool, and to
hear it bickering away in its rusty channel. But
the beauty of the place is not a simple beauty;
there is something strange and almost fierce about
the red-stained water-course; something uncanny
and terrifying about the filmy orange clouds that
stir and sway in the pool; and there sleeps, too,
round the edges of the basin a bright and viscous
scum, with a certain ugly radiance, shot with
colours that are almost too sharp and fervid for
nature. It seems as though some diligent alchemy
was at work, pouring out from moment to moment
this strangely tempered potion. In summer it is
more bearable to look upon, when the grass is
bright and soft, when the tapestry of leaves and
climbing plants is woven over the skirts of the
thicket, when the trees are in joyful leaf. But in
the winter, when all tints are low and spare, when
the pastures are yellowed with age, and the hill-side
wrinkled with cold, when the alder-rods stand up
stiff and black, and the leafless tangled boughs are
smooth like wire; then the pool has a certain horror,
as it pours out its rich juice, all overhung with thin
steam.

But I doubt not that I read into it some thoughts

of my own; for it was on such a day of winter, when the sky was full of inky clouds, and the wood murmured like a falling sea in the buffeting wind, that I made a grave and sad decision beside the red pool, that has since tinged my life, as the orange waters tinge the pale stream into which they fall. The shadow of that severe resolve still broods about the place for me.   How often since in thought have I threaded the meadows, and looked with the inward eye upon the green water rising, rising, and the crowded orange-fleeces of the pool!   But stern though the resolve was, it was not an unhappy one; and it has brought into my life a firm and tonic quality, which seems to me to hold within it something of the astringent savour of the medicated waters, and perhaps something of their health-giving powers as well.

II

I was making a vague pilgrimage to-day in a distant and unfamiliar part of the country, a region that few people ever visit, and saw two things that moved me strangely.   I left the high-road to explore a hamlet that lay down in a broad valley to the left; and again diverged from the beaten track to survey an old grange that lay at a little distance among the fields.   Turning a corner by some cottages, I saw a small ancient chapel, of brown weathered stone, covered with orange lichen, the roof of rough stone tiles.   In the narrow graveyard round it, the grass grew long and rank; the gateway was choked by briars.   I could see that the windows of the tiny building were broken.   I have never before in England seen a derelict church, and I clambered over the wall to examine it more closely. It stood very beautifully; from the low wall of the graveyard, on the further side, you could look over a wide extent of rich water-meadows, fed by full streams; there was much ranunculus in flower on the edges of the watercourses, and a few cattle moved leisurely about with a peaceful air.   Far over the meadows, out of a small grove of trees, a manor-house held up its enquiring chimneys.   The door of the chapel was open, and I have seldom seen a more pitiful sight than it revealed.   The roof within was of a plain and beautiful design, with carved bosses, and beams of some dark wood. The chapel was fitted with oak Jacobean woodwork, pews, a reading-desk, and a little screen.   At the west was a tiny balustraded gallery.   But the whole was a scene of wretched confusion.   The woodwork was mouldering, the red cloth of the pulpit hung raggedly down, the leaves of the great prayer-book fluttered about the pavement, in the draught from the door. The whole place was gnawed by rats and shockingly befouled by birds; there was a litter of rotting nests upon the altar itself. Yet in the walls were old memorial tablets, and the passage of the nave was paved with lettered graves. It brought back to me the beautiful lines—

> " En ara, ramis ilicis obsita,
> Quae sacra Chryses nomina fert deae,
> Neglecta; jamdudum sepultus
> Aedituus jacet et sacerdos."

Outside the sun fell peacefully on the mellow walls, and the starlings twittered in the roof; but inside the deserted shrine there was a sense of broken trust, of old memories despised, of the altar of God shamed and dishonoured. It was a pious design to build the little chapel there for the secluded hamlet; and loving thought and care had gone to making the place seemly and beautiful. The very stone of the wall, and the beam of the roof cried out against the hard and untender usage that had laid the sanctuary low. Here children had been baptized, tender marriage vows plighted, and the dead laid to rest; and this was the end. I turned away with a sense of deep sadness; the very sunshine seemed blurred with a shadow of dreariness and shame.

Then I made my way, by a stony road, towards

the manor-house; and presently could see its gables
at the end of a pleasant avenue of limes; but no
track led thither.   The gate was wired up, and the
drive overgrown with grass.   Soon, however, I
found a farm-road which led up to the house from
the village.   On the left of the manor lay prosperous barns and byres, full of sleek pigs and busy
crested fowls.   The teams came clanking home
across the water-meadows.   The house itself became more and more beautiful as I approached.   It
was surrounded by a moat, and here, close at hand,
stood another ancient chapel, in seemly repair.   All
round the house grew dense thickets of sprawling
laurels, which rose in luxuriance from the edge of
the water.   Then I crossed a little bridge with a
broken parapet; and in front of me stood the house
itself.   I have seldom seen a more perfectly proportioned or exquisitely coloured building.   There
were three gables in the front, the central one holding a beautiful oriel window, with a fine oak door
below.   The whole was built of a pale red brick,
covered with a grey lichen that cast a shimmering
light over the front.   Tall chimneys of solid grace
rose from a stone-shingled roof.   The coigns,
parapets and mullions were all of a delicately-
tinted orange stone.   To the right lay a big walled
garden, full of flowers growing with careless richness, the whole bounded by the moat, and looking

out across the broad green water-meadows, beyond
which the low hills rose softly in gentle curves and
dingles.

A whole company of amiable dogs, spaniels and
terriers, came out with an effusive welcome; a big
black yard-dog, after a loud protesting bark,
joined in the civilities. And there I sat down in
the warm sun, to drink in the beauty of the scene,
while the moor-hens cried plaintively in the moat,
and the dogs disposed themselves at my feet. The
man who designed this old place must have had a
wonderful sense of the beauty of proportion, the
charm of austere simplicity. Generation after
generation must have loved the gentle dignified
house, with its narrow casements, its high rooms.
Though the name of the house, though the tale of
its dwellers was unknown to me, I felt the appeal
of the old associations that must have centred about
it. The whole air, that quiet afternoon, seemed
full of the calling of forgotten voices, and dead
faces looked out from the closed lattices. So near
to my heart came the spirit of the ancient house,
that, as I mused, I felt as though even I myself
had made a part of its past, and as though I were
returning from battling with the far-off world to
the home of childhood. The house seemed to regard me with a mournful and tender gaze, as
though it knew that I loved it, and would fain utter

its secrets in a friendly ear. Is it strange that a
thing of man's construction should have so wistful
yet so direct a message for the spirit? Well, I
hardly know what it was that it spoke of; but I felt
the care and love that had gone to the making of it,
and the dignity that it had won from rain and sun
and the kindly hand of Nature; it spoke of hope
and brightness, of youth and joy; and told me, too,
that all things were passing away, that even the
house itself, though it could outlive a few restless
generations, was indeed *debita morti,* and bowed
itself to its fall.

And then I too, like a bird of passage that has
alighted for a moment in some sheltered garden-
ground, must needs go on my way. But the old
house had spoken with me, had left its mark upon
my spirit. And I know that in weary hours, far
hence, I shall remember how it stood, peering out
of its tangled groves, gazing at the sunrise and the
sunset over the green flats, waiting for what may
be, and dreaming of the days that are no more.

III

I HAVE had a taste, during the last few days, I
know not why, of the cup of what Gray called
Leucocholy; it is not Melancholy, only the pale

shadow of it. That dark giant is, doubtless, stalking somewhere in the background, and the shadow cast by his misshapen head passes over my little garden ground.

I do not readily submit to this mood, and I would wish it away. I would rather feel joyful and free from blame; but Gray called it a good easy state, and it certainly has its compensations. It does not, like Melancholy, lay a dark hand on duties and pleasures alike; it is possible to work, to read, to talk, to laugh when it is by. But it sends flowing through the mind a gentle current of sad and weary images and thoughts, which still have a beauty of their own; it tinges one's life with a sober greyness of hue; it heightens perception, though it prevents enjoyment. In such a mood one can sit silent a long time, with one's eyes cast upon the grass; one sees the delicate forms of the tender things that spring softly out of the dark ground; one hears with a piognant delight the clear notes of birds; something of the spring languors move within the soul. There is a sense, too, of reaching out to light and joy, a stirring of the vague desires of the heart, a tender hope, an upward-climbing faith; the heart sighs for a peace that it cannot attain.

To-day I walked slowly and pensively by little woods and pastures, taking delight in all the quiet life I saw, the bush pricked with points of green, the boughs thickened with small reddening buds, the slow stream moving through the pasture; all the tints faint, airy, and delicate; the life of the world seemed to hang suspended, waiting for the forward leap. In a little village I stood awhile to watch the gables of an ancient house, the wing of a ruined grange, peer solemnly over the mellow brick wall that guarded a close of orchard trees. A little way behind, the blunt pinnacles of the old church-tower stood up, blue and dim, over the branching elms; beyond all ran the long, pure line of the rising wold. Everything seemed so still, so serene, as a long, pale ray of the falling sun, which laboured among flying clouds, touched the westward gables with gold—and mine the only troubled, unquiet spirit. Hard by there was an old man tottering about in a little garden, fumbling with some plants, like Laertes on the upland farm. His worn face, his ragged beard, his pitifully-patched and creased garments made him a very type of an ineffectual sadness. Perhaps his thoughts ran as sadly as my own, but I do not think it was so, because the minds of many country-people, and of almost all the old, of whatever degree, seem to me free from what is the curse of delicately-trained and highly-strung temperaments—namely, the temptation to be always reverting to the past, or forecasting the future. Simple people and aged people put that aside, and live quite serenely in the moment; and that is what I believe we ought all to attempt, for most moments are bearable, if one only does not import into them the weight of the future and the regret of the past. To seize the moment with all its conditions, to press the quality out if it, that is the best victory. But, alas! we are so made that though we may know that a course is the wise, the happy, the true course, we cannot always pursue it. I remember a story of a public man who bore his responsibilities very hardly, worried and agonised over him, saying to Mr. Gladstone, who was at that time in the very thick of a fierce political crisis: " But don't you find you lie awake at night, thinking how you ought to act, and how you ought to have acted? " Mr. Gladstone turned his great, flashing eyes upon his interlocutor, and said, with a look of wonder: " No, I don't; where would be the use of that? " And again I remember that old Canon Beadon—who lived, I think, to his 104th year—said to a friend that the secret of long life in his own case was that he had never thought of anything unpleasant after ten o'clock at night. Of course, if you have a series of compartments in your brain, and at ten o'clock can turn the key quietly upon the room that holds the skeletons and nightmares, you are a very fortunate man.

But still, we can all of us do something. If one has the courage and good sense, when in a melancholy mood, to engage in some piece of practical work, it is wonderful how one can distract the great beast that, left to himself, crops and munches the tender herbage of the spirit. For myself I have generally a certain number of dull tasks to perform, not in themselves interesting, and out of which little pleasure can be extracted, except the pleasure which always results from finishing a piece of necessary work. When I am wise, I seize upon a day in which I am overhung with a shadow of sadness to clear off work of this kind. It is in itself a distraction, and then one has the pleasure both of having fought the mood and also of having left the field clear for the mind, when it has recovered its tone, to settle down firmly and joyfully to more congenial labours.

To-day, little by little, the cloudy mood drew off and left me smiling. The love of the peaceful and patient earth came to comfort me. How pure and free were the long lines of ploughland, the broad back of the gently-swelling down! How clear and delicate were the February tints, the aged grass, the leafless trees! What a sense of coolness and repose! I stopped a long time upon a rustic-timbered bridge to look at a little stream that ran beneath the road, winding down through a rough

pasture-field, with many thorn-thickets. The water, lapsing slowly through withered flags, had the
pure, gem-like quality of the winter stream; in summer it will become dim and turbid with infusorial
life, but now it is like a pale jewel. How strange,
I thought, to think of this liquid gaseous juice,
which we call water, trickling in the cracks of the
earth! And just as the fish that live in it think of
it as their world, and have little cognisance of
what happens in the acid, unsubstantial air above,
except the occasional terror of the dim, looming
forms which come past, making the soft banks
quiver and stir, so it may be with us; there may be
a great mysterious world outside of us, of which
we sometimes see the dark manifestations, and yet
of the conditions of which we are wholly
unaware.

And now it grew dark; the horizon began to
redden and smoulder; the stream gleamed like a
wan thread among the distant fields. It was time
to hurry home, to dip in the busy tide of life again.
Where was my sad mood gone? The clear air
seemed to have blown through my mind, hands had
been waved to me from leafless woods, quiet voices
of field and stream had whispered me their secrets;
"We would tell, if we could," they seemed to say.
And I, listening, had learned patience, too—for
awhile.

IV

I HAVE made friends with a new flower. If it
had a simple and wholesome English name, I would
like to know it, though I do not care to know what
ugly and clumsy title the botany books may give
it; but it lives in my mind, a perfect and complete
memory of brightness and beauty, and, as I have
said, a friend.

It was in a steep sea-cove that I saw it. Round
a small circular basin of blue sea ran up gigantic
cliffs, grey limestone bluffs; here and there, where
they were precipitous, slanted the monstrous wavy
lines of distorted strata, thrust up, God alone knows
how many ages ago, by some sharp and horrible
shiver of the boiling earth. Little waves broke on
the pebbly beach at our feet, and all the air was full
of pleasant sharp briny savours. A few boats were
drawn up on the shingle; lobster-pots, nets, strings
of cork, spars, oars, lay in pleasant confusion, by
the sandy road that led up to the tiny hamlet above.
We had travelled far that day and were comfort-
ably weary; we found a sloping ledge of turf upon
which we sat, and presently became aware that on
the little space of grass between us and the cliff
must once have stood a cottage and a cottage garden. There was a broken wall behind us, and the
little platform still held some garden flowers

sprawling wildly, a stunted fruit-bush or two, a knotted apple-tree.

My own flower, or the bushes on which it grew, had once, I think, formed part of the cottage ledge; but it had found a wider place to its liking, for it ran riot everywhere; it scaled the cliff, where, too, the golden wall-flowers of the garden had gained a footing; it fringed the sandpatches beyond us, it rooted itself firmly in the shingle. The plant had rough light-brown branches, which were now all starred with the greenest tufts imaginable; but the flower itself! On many of the bushes it was not yet fully out, and showed only in an abundance of small lilac balls, carefully folded; but just below me a cluster had found the sun and the air too sweet to resist, and had opened to the light. The flower was of a delicate veined purple, a five-pointed star, with a soft golden heart. All the open blossoms stared at me with a tranquil gaze, knowing I would not hurt them.

Below, two fishermen rowed a boat quietly out to sea, the sharp creaking of the rowlocks coming lazily to our ears in the pauses of the wind. The little waves fell with a soft thud, followed by the crisp echo of the surf, feeling all round the shingly cove. The whole place, in that fresh spring day, was unutterably peaceful and content.

And I too forgot all my busy schemes and hopes

and aims, the tiny part I play in the world, with so much petty energy, such anxious responsibility. My purple-starred flower approved of my acquiescence, smiling trustfully upon me. "Here," it seemed to say, "I bloom and brighten, spring after spring. No one regards me, no one cares for me; no one praises my beauty; no one sorrows when these leaves grow pale, when I fall from my stem, when my dry stalks whisper together in the winter wind. But to you, because you have seen and loved me, I whisper my secret." And then the flower told me something that I cannot write even if I would, because it is in the language unspeakable, of which St. Paul wrote that such words are not lawful for a man to utter; but they are heard in the third heaven of God.

Then I felt that if I could but remember what the flower said I should never grieve or strive or be sorrowful any more; but, as the wise Psalmist said, be content to tarry the Lord's leisure. Yet, even when I thought that I had the words by heart, they ceased like a sweet music that comes to an end, and which the mind cannot recover.

I saw many other things that day, things beautiful and wonderful, no doubt; but they had no voice for me, like the purple flower; or if they had, the sea wind drowned them in the utterance, for their voices were of the earth; but the flower's voice came, as I have said, from the innermost heaven.

I like well to go on pilgrimage; and in spite of weariness and rainy weather, and the stupid chatter of the men and women who congregate like fowls in inn-parlours, I pile a little treasure of sights and sounds in my guarded heart, memories of old buildings, spring woods, secluded valleys. All these are things seen, impressions registered and gratefully recorded. But my flower is somehow different from all these; and I shall never again hear the name of the place mentioned, or even see a map of that grey coast, without a quiet thrill of gladness at the thought that there, spring by spring, blooms my little friend, whose heart I read, who told me its secret; who will wait for me to return, and indeed will be faithfully and eternally mine, whether I return or no.

V

I HAVE lately become convinced—and I do not say it either sophistically, to plead a bad cause with dexterity, or resignedly, to make the best out of a poor business; but with a true and hearty conviction—that the most beautiful country in England is the flat fenland. I do not here mean moderately

flat country, low sweeps of land, like the heaving
of a dying groundswell; that has a miniature
beauty, a stippled delicacy of its own, but it is not
a fine quality of charm.   The country that I would
praise is the rigidly and mathematically flat country of Eastern England, lying but a few feet above
the sea plains which were once the bottoms of huge
and ancient swamps.

In the first place, such country gives a wonderful sense of expanse and space; from an eminence
of a few feet you can see what in other parts of
England you have to climb a considerable hill to
discern.   I love to feast my eyes on the intermin-
able rich level plain, with its black and crumbling
soil; the long simple lines of dykes and water-
courses carry the eye peacefully out to a great
distance; then, too, by having all the landscape compressed into so narrow a space, into a belt of what
is, to the eye, only a few inches in depth, you get
an incomparable richness of colour.   The solitary
distant clumps of trees surrounding a lonely farm
gain a deep intensity of tint from the vast green
level all about them; and the line of the low far-off
wolds, that close the view many miles away, is of
a peculiar delicacy and softness; the eye, too, is
provided with a foreground of which the elements
are of the simplest; a reedy pool enclosed by wil-
lows, the clustered buildings of a farmstead; a grey

church-tower peering out over churchyard elms;
and thus, instead of being checked by near objects,
and hemmed in by the limited landscape, the eye
travels out across the plain with a sense of freedom
and grateful repose. Then, too, there is the huge
perspective of the sky; nowhere else is it possible
to see, so widely, the slow march of clouds from
horizon to horizon; it all gives a sense of largeness
and tranquillity such as you receive upon the sea,
with the additional advantage of having the solid
earth beneath you, green and fertile, instead of the
steely waste of waters.

A day or two ago I found myself beside the
lower waters of the Cam, in flat pastures, full of
ancient thorn-trees just bursting into bloom. I
gained the towing-path, which led me out gradually
into the heart of the fen; the river ran, or rather
moved, a sapphire streak, between its high green
flood-banks; the wide spaces between the embanked
path and the stream were full of juicy herbage,
great tracts of white cow-parsley, with here and
there a reed-bed. I stood long to listen to the
sharp song of the reed-warbler, slipping from
spray to spray of a willow-patch. Far to the north
the great tower of Ely rose blue and dim above
the low lines of trees; in the centre of the pastures
lay the long brown line of the sedge-beds of Wicken
Mere, almost the only untouched tract of fenland;

slow herds of cattle grazed, more and more minute, in the unhedged pasture-land, and the solitary figure of a labourer moving homeward on the top of the green dyke, seemed in the long afternoon to draw no nearer. Here and there were the floodgates of a lode, with the clear water slowly spilling itself over the rim of the sluice, full of floating weed. There was something infinitely reposeful in the solitude, the width of the landscape; there was no sense of crowded life, no busy figures, intent on their small aims, to cross one's path, no conflict, no strife, no bitterness, no insistent voice; yet there was no sense of desolation, but rather the spectacle of glad and simple lives of plants and birds in the free air, their wildness tamed by the far-off and controlling hand of man, the calm earth patiently serving his ends. I seemed to have passed out of modern life into a quieter and older world, before men congregated into cities, but lived the quiet and sequestered life of the country-side; and little by little there stole into my heart something of a dreamful tranquility, the calm of the slow brimming stream, the leisurely herds, the growing grass. All seemed to be moving together, neither lingering nor making haste, to some far-off end within the quiet mind of God. Everything seemed to be waiting, musing, living the untroubled life of nature, with no thought of death or care or sorrow. I

passed a trench of still water that ran as far as the
eye could follow it across the flat; it was full from
end to end of the beautiful water-violet, the pale
lilac flowers, with their faint ethereal scent, clustered on the head of a cool emerald spike, with the
rich foliage of the plant, like fine green hair, filling
the water. The rising of these beautiful forms, by
some secret consent, in their appointed place and
time, out of the fresh clear water, brought me a
wistful sense of peace and order, a desire for I
hardly know what—a poised stateliness of life, a
tender beauty—if I could but win it for myself!

On and on, hour by hour, that still bright afternoon, I made my slow way over the fen; insensibly
and softly the far-off villages fell behind; and yet
I seemed to draw no nearer to the hills of the horizon. Now and then I passed a lonely grange;
once or twice I came near to a tall shuttered en-
gine-house of pale brick, and heard the slow beat
of the pumps within, like the pulse of a hidden
heart, which drew the marsh-water from a hundred
runlets, and poured it slowly seawards. Field after
field slid past me, some golden from end to end
with buttercups, some waving with young wheat,
till at last I reached a solitary inn beside a ferry,
with the quaint title: " *No hurry ! five miles from
anywhere.*" And here I met with a grave and
kindly welcome, such as warms the heart of one

who goes on pilgrimage: as though I was certainly expected, and as if the lord of the place had given charge concerning me. It would indeed hardly have surprised me if I had been had into a room, and shown strange symbols of good and evil; or if I had been given a roll and a bottle, and a note of the way. But no such presents were made to me, and it was not until after I had left the little house, and had been ferried in an old blackened boat across the stream, that I found that I had the gifts in my bosom all the while.

The roll was the fair sight that I had seen, in this world where it is so sweet to live. My cordial was the peace within my spirit. And as for the way, it seemed plain enough that day, easy to discern and follow; and the heavenly city itself as near and visible as the blue towers that rose so solemnly upon the green horizon.

VI

IT is not often that one is fortunate enough to see two perfectly beautiful things in one day. But such was my fortune in the late summer, on a day that was in itself perfect enough to show what September can do, if he only has a mind to plan hours of delight for man. The distance was very blue and marvellously clear. The trees had the bronzed look of the summer's end, with deep azure shadows. The cattle moved slowly about the fields, and there was harvesting going on, so that the villages we passed seemed almost deserted. I will not say whence we started or where we went, and I shall mention no names at all, except one, which is of the nature of a symbol or incantation; for I do not desire that others should go where I went, unless I could be sure that they went with the same peace in their hearts that I bore with me that day.

One of the places we visited on purpose; the other we saw by accident. On the small map we carried was marked, at the corner of a little wood that seemed to have no way to it, a well with the name of a saint, of whom I never heard, though I doubt not she is written in the book of God.

We reached the nearest point to the well upon the road, and we struck into the fields; that was a sweet place where we found ourselves! In ancient days it had been a marsh, I think. For great ditches ran everywhere, choked with loose-strife and water-dock, and the ground quaked as we walked, a pleasant springy black mould, the dust of endless centuries of the rich water plants.

To the left, the ground ran up sharply in a minute bluff, with the soft outline of underlying chalk, covered with small thorn-thickets; and it was all

encircled with small, close woods, where we heard
the pheasants scamper. We found an old, slow,
bovine man, with a cheerful face, who readily threw
aside some fumbling work he was doing, and
guided us; and we should never have found the spot
without him. He led us to a stream, crossed by a
single plank with a handrail, on which some children had put a trap, baited with nuts for the poor
squirrels, that love to run chattering across the rail
from wood to wood. Then we entered a little
covert; it was very pleasant in there, all dark and
green and still; and here all at once we came to the
place; in the covert were half a dozen little steep
pits, each a few yards across, dug out of the chalk.
From each of the pits, which lay side by side, a
channel ran down to the stream, and in each channel flowed a small bickering rivulet of infinite clearness. The pits themselves were a few feet deep; at
the bottom of each was a shallow pool, choked with
leaves; and here lay the rare beauty of the place.
The water rose in each pit out of secret ways, but
in no place that we could see. The first pit was
still when we looked upon it; then suddenly the water rose in a tiny eddy, in one corner, among the
leaves, sending a little ripple glancing across the
pool. It was as though something, branch or in-
sect, had fallen from above, the water leapt so
suddenly. Then it rose again in another place,

then in another; then five or six little freshets rose
all at once, the rings crossing and recrossing. And
it was the same in all the pits, which we visited one
by one; we descended and drank, and found the
water as cold as ice, and not less pure; while the
old man babbled on about the waste of so much
fine water, and of its virtues for weak eyes: "Ain't
it cold, now? Ain't it, then? My God, ain't it?"
—he was a man with a rich store of simple assever-
ations,—"And ain't it good for weak eyes neither!
You must just come to the place the first thing in
the morning, and wash your eyes in the water, and
ain't it strengthening then!" So he chirped on,
saying everything over and over, like a bird among
the thickets.

We paid him for his trouble, with a coin that
made him so gratefully bewildered that he said to
us: "Now, gentlemen, if there's anything else that
you want, give it a name; and if you meet any one
as you go away, say 'Perrett told me' (Perrett's
my name), and then you'll see!" What the precise virtue of this invocation was, we did not have
an opportunity of testing, but that it was a talis-
man to unlock hidden doors, I make no doubt.

We went back silently over the fields, with the
wonder of the thing still in our minds. To think
of the pure wells bubbling and flashing, by day and
by night, in the hot summer weather, when the

smell of the wood lies warm in the sun; on cold winter nights under moon and stars, forever casting up the bright elastic jewel, that men call water, and feeding the flowing stream that wanders to the sea. I was very full of gratitude to the pure maiden saint that lent her name to the well, and I am sure she never had a more devout pair of worshippers.

So we sped on in silence, thinking—at least I thought—how the water leaped and winked in the sacred wells, and how clear showed the chalk, and the leaves that lay at the bottom: till at last we drew to our other goal. " Here is the gate," said my companion at last.

On one side of the road stood a big substantial farm; on the other, by a gate, was a little lodge. Here a key was given us by an old hearty man, with plenty of advice of a simple and sententious kind, until I felt as though I were enacting a part in some little *Pilgrim's Progress,* and as if *Mr. Interpreter* himself, with a very grave smile, would come out and have me into a room by myself, to see some odd pleasant show that he had provided. But it was perhaps more in the manner of *Evangelist,* for our guide pointed with his finger across a very wide field, and showed us a wicket to enter in at.

Here was a great flat grassy pasture, the water

3

again very near the surface, as the long-leaved water-plants, that sprawled in all the ditches, showed.
But when we reached the wicket we seemed to be
as far removed from humanity as dwellers in a
lonely isle. A few cattle grazed drowsily, and the
crisp tearing of the grass by their big lips came
softly across the pasture. Inside the wicket stood
a single ancient house, uninhabited, and festooned
with ivy into a thing more bush than house; though
a small Tudor window peeped from the leaves, like
the little suspicious eye of some shaggy beast.

A stone's throw away lay a large square moat,
full of water, all fringed with ancient gnarled
trees; the island which it enclosed was overgrown
with tiny thickets of dishevelled box-trees, and
huge sprawling laurels; we walked softly round it,
and there was our goal: a small church of a whitish
stone, in the middle of a little close of old sycamores
in stiff summer leaf.

It stood so remote, so quietly holy, so ancient,
that I could think of nothing but the "old febel
chapel" of the *Morte d' Arthur.* It had, I know
not why, the mysterious air of romance all about it.
It seemed to sit, musing upon what had been and
what should be, smilingly guarding some tender
secret for the pure-hearted, full of the peace the
world cannot give.

Within it was cool and dark, and had an ancient

holy smell; it was furnished sparely with seat and screen, and held monuments of old knights and ladies, sleeping peacefully side by side, heads pillowed on hands, looking out with quiet eyes, as though content to wait.

Upon the island in the moat, we learned, had stood once a flourishing manor, but through what sad vicissitudes it had fallen into dust I care not. Enough that peaceful lives had been lived there; children had been born, had played on the moat-edge, had passed away to bear children of their own, had returned with love in their hearts for the old house. From the house to the church children had been borne for baptism; merry wedding processions had gone to and fro, happy Christmas groups had hurried backwards and forwards; and the slow funeral pomp had passed thither, under the beating of the slow bell, bearing one that should not return.

Something of the love and life and sorrow of the good days passed into my mind, and I gave a tender thought to men and women whom I had never known, who had tasted of life, and of joyful things that have an end; and who now know the secret of the dark house to which we all are bound.

When we at last rose unwillingly to go, the sun was setting, and flamed red and brave through the gnarled trunks of the little wood; the mist crept

over the pasture, and far away the lights of the
lonely farm began to wink through the gathering
dark.

But I had seen! Something of the joy of the
two sweet places had settled in my mind; and now,
in fretful, weary, wakeful hours, it is good to think
of the clear wells that sparkle so patiently in the
dark wood; and, better still, to wander in mind
about the moat and the little silent church; and to
wonder what it all means; what the love is that
creeps over the soul at the sight of these places, so
full of a remote and delicate beauty; and whether
the hunger of the heart for peace and permanence,
which visits us so often in our short and difficult
pilgrimage, has a counterpart in the land that is
very far off.

VII

I HAVE been much haunted, indeed infested, if
the word may be pardoned, by cuckoos lately;
When I was a child, acute though my observation
of birds and beasts and natural things was, I do
not recollect that I ever saw a cuckoo, though I
often tried to stalk one by the ear, following the
sweet siren melody, as it dropped into the expectant
silence from a hedgerow tree; and I remember to

have heard the notes of two, that seemed to answer each other, draw closer each time they called.

But of late I have become familiar with the silvery grey body and the gliding flight; and this year I have been almost dogged by them. One flew beside me, as I rode the other day, for nearly a quarter of a mile along a hedgerow, taking short gliding flights, and settling till I came up; I could see his shimmering wings and his long barred tail. I dismounted at last, and he let me watch him for a long time, noting his small active head, his decent sober coat. Then, when he thought I had seen enough, he gave one rich bell-like call, with the full force of his soft throat, and floated off.

He seemed loath to leave me. But what word or gift, I thought, did he bring with him, false and pretty bird? Do I too desire that others should hatch my eggs, content with flute-like notes of pleasure?

And yet how strange and marvellous a thing this instinct is; that one bird, by an absolute and unvarying instinct, should forego the dear business of nesting and feeding, and should take shrewd advantage of the labours of other birds! It cannot be a deliberately reasoned or calculated thing; at least we say that it cannot; and yet not Darwin and all his followers have brought us any nearer to the method by which such an instinct is developed and trained, till it has become an absolute law of the tribe; making it as natural a thing for the cuckoo to search for a built nest, and to cast away its foundling egg there, as it is for other birds to welcome and feed the intruder. It seems so satanically clever a thing to do; such a strange fantastic whim of the Creator to take thought in originating it! It is this whimsicality, the *bizarre* humour in Nature, that puzzles me more than anything in the world, because it seems like the sport of a child with odd inconsequent fancies, and with omnipotence behind it all the time. It seems strange enough to think of the laws that govern the breeding, nesting, and nurture of birds at all, especially when one considers all the accidents that so often make the toil futile, like the stealing of eggs by other birds, and the predatory incursions of foes. One would expect a law, framed by omnipotence, to be invariable, not hampered by all kinds of difficulties that omnipotence, one might have thought, could have provided against. And then comes this further strange variation in the law, in the case of this single family of birds, and the mystery thickens and deepens. And stranger than all is the existence of the questioning and unsatisfied human spirit, that observes these things and classifies them, and that yet gets no nearer to the solution of the huge, fantastic, patient plan! To make a law, as the Creator seems to have done; and then to make a hundred other laws that seem to make the first law inoperative; to play this gigantic game century after century; and then to put into the hearts of our inquisitive race the desire to discover what it is all about; and to leave the desire unsatisfied. What a labyrinthine mystery! Depth beyond depth, and circle beyond circle!

It is a dark and bewildering region that thus opens to the view. But one conclusion is to beware of seeming certainties, to keep the windows of the mind open to the light; not to be over-anxious about the little part we have to play in the great pageant, but to advance, step by step, in utter trustfulness.

Perhaps that is your message to me, graceful bird, with the rich joyful note! With what a thrill, too, do you bring back to me the brightness of old forgotten springs, the childish rapture at the sweet tunable cry! Then, in those far-off days, it was but the herald of the glowing summer days, the time of play and flowers and scents. But now the soft note, it seems, opens a door into the formless and uneasy world of speculation, of questions that have no answer, convincing me of ignorance and doubt, bidding me beat in vain against the bars that hem me in. Why should I crave thus for certainty, for strength? Answer me, happy bird!

Nay, you guard your secret.   Softer and more distant sound the sweet notes, warning me to rest and believe, telling me to wait and hope.

But one further thought!   One is expected, by people of conventional or orthodox minds, to base one's conceptions of God on the writings of frail and fallible men, and to accept their slender and eager testimony to the occurrence of abnormal events as the best revelation of God that the world contains.   And all the while we disregard his own patient writing upon the wall.   Every day and every hour we are confronted with strange marvels, which we dismiss from our minds because, God forgive us, we call them natural; and yet they take us back, by a ladder of immeasurable antiquity, to ages before man had emerged from a savage state.   Centuries before our rude forefathers had learned even to scratch a few hillocks into earthworks, while they lived a brutish life, herding in dens and caves, the cuckoo, with her traditions faultlessly defined, was paying her annual visits, fluting about the forest glades, and searching for nests into which to intrude her speckled egg.   The patient witness of God!   She is as direct a revelation of the Creator's mind, could we but interpret the mystery of her instincts, as Augustine himself with his scheme of salvation logically defined.   Each of these missions, whether of bird or man, a wonder and a mar-

vel! But do we not tend to accept the eager and
childish hopes of humanity, arrayed with blithe certainty, as a nearer evidence of the mind of God
than the bird that at his bidding pursues her annual quest, unaffected by our hasty conclusions,
unmoved by our glorified visions? I have sometimes thought that Christ probably spoke more
than is recorded about the observation of Nature;
the hearts of those that heard him were so set on
temporal ends and human applications, that they
had not perhaps leisure or capacity to recollect
aught but those few scattered words, that seem to
speak of a deep love for and insight into the things
of earth. They remembered better that Christ
blasted a fig-tree for not doing what the Father bade
the poor plant do, than his tender dwelling upon
grasses and lilies, sparrow and sheep. The withering of the tree made an allegory: while the love of
flowers and streams was to those simple hearts perhaps an unaccountable, almost an eccentric thing.
But had Christ drawn human breath in our bleaker
Northern air, he would have perhaps, if those that
surrounded him had had leisure and grace to listen,
drawn as grave and comforting a soul-music from
our homely cuckoo, with her punctual obedience,
her unquestioning faith, as he did from the birds
and flowers of the hot hillsides, the pastoral valleys
of Palestine. I am sure he would have loved the

cuckoo, and forgiven her her heartless customs. Those that sing so delicately would not have leisure and courage to make their music so soft and sweet, if they had not a hard heart to turn to the sorrows of the world.

Yet still I am no nearer the secret. God sends me, here the frozen peak, there the blue sea; here the tiger, there the cuckoo; here Virgil, there Jeremiah; here St. Francis of Assisi, there Napoleon. And all the while, as he pushes his fair or hurtful toys upon the stage, not a whisper, not a smile, not a glance escapes him; he thrusts them on, he lays them by; but the interpretation he leaves with us, and there is never a word out of the silence to show us whether we have guessed aright.

VIII

YESTERDAY was a day of brisk airs. The wind was at work brushing great inky clouds out of the sky. They came sailing up, those great rounded masses of dark vapour, like huge galleons driving to the West, spilling their freight as they came. The air would be suddenly full of tall twisted rain-streaks, and then would come a bright burst of the sun.

But a secret change came in the night; some silent power filled the air with warmth and balm.

And to-day, when I walked out of the town with an old and familiar friend, the spring had come. A maple had broken into bloom and leaf; a chestnut was unfolding his gummy buds; the cottage gardens were full of squills and hepatica; and the mezereons were all thick with damask buds. In green and sheltered underwoods there were bursts of daffodils; hedges were pricked with green points; and a delicate green tapestry was beginning to weave itself over the roadside ditches.

The air seemed full of a deep content. Birds fluted softly, and the high elms which stirred in the wandering breezes were all thick with their red buds. There was so much to look at and to point out that we talked but fitfully; and there was, too, a gentle languor abroad which made us content to be silent.

In one village which we passed, a music-loving squire had made a concert for his friends and neighbours, and doubtless, too, for our vagrant delight; we stood uninvited to listen to a tuneful stir of violins, which with a violoncello booming beneath, broke out very pleasantly from the windows of a village school-room.

When body and mind are fresh and vigorous, these outside impressions often lose, I think, their sharp savours. One is preoccupied with one's own happy schemes and merry visions; the bird sings

shrill within its cage, and claps its golden wings.
But on such soft and languorous days as these days
of early spring, when the body is unstrung, and the
bonds and ties that fasten the soul to its prison are
loosened and unbound, the spirit, striving to be
glad, draws in through the passages of sense these
swift impressions of beauty, as a thirsty child
drains a cup of spring-water on a sun-scorched
day, lingering over the limpid freshness of the gliding element. The airy voices of the strings being
stilled, with a sort of pity for those penned in the
crowded room, interchanging the worn coinage of
civility, we stood a while looking in at a gate,
through which we could see the cool front of a
Georgian manor-house, built of dusky bricks, with
coigns and dressings of grey stone. The dark
windows with their thick white casements, the
round-topped dormers, the steps up to the door,
and a prim circle of grass which seemed to lie like
a carpet on the pale gravel, gave the feeling of a
picture; the whole being framed in the sombre yews
of shrubberies which bordered the drive. It was
hard to feel that the quiet house was the scene of a
real and active life; it seemed so full of a slumber-
ous peace, and to be tenanted only by soft shadows
of the past. And so we went slowly on by the huge
white-boarded mill, its cracks streaming with
congealed dust of wheat, where the water thun-

dered through the sluices and the gear rattled
within.

We crossed the bridge, and walked on by a field-
track that skirted the edge of the wold. How thin
and clean were the tints of the dry ploughlands and
the long sweep of pasture! Presently we were at
the foot of a green drift-road, an old Roman highway that ran straight up into the downs. On such
a day as this, one follows a spirit in one's feet, as
Shelley said; and we struck up into the wold, on
the green road, with its thorn-thickets, until the
chalk began to show white among the ruts; and we
were soon at the top. A little to the left of us appeared, in the middle of the pasture, a tiny round-
topped tumulus that I had often seen from a lower
road, but never visited. It was fresher and cooler
up here. On arriving at the place we found that
it was not a tumulus at all, but a little out-
crop of the pure chalk. It had steep, scarped
sides with traces of caves scooped in them. The
grassy top commanded a wide view of wold and
plain.

Our talk wandered over many things, but here,
I do not know why, we were speaking of the taking
up of old friendships, and the comfort and delight
of those serene and undisturbed relations which one
sometimes establishes with a congenial person,
which no lapse of time or lack of communication

seems to interrupt—the best kind of friendship. There is here no blaming of conditions that may keep the two lives apart; no feverish attempt to keep up the relation, no resentment if mutual intercourse dies away. And then, perhaps, in the shifting of conditions, one's life is again brought near to the life of one's friend, and the old easy intercourse is greatly resumed. My companion said that such a relation seemed to him to lie as near to the solution of the question of the preservation of identity after death as any other phenomenon of life. "Supposing," he said, "that such a friendship as that of which we have spoken is resumed after a break of twenty years. One is in no respect the same person; one looks different, one's views of life have altered, and physiologists tell us that one's body has changed perhaps three times over, in the time so that there is not a particle of our frame that is the same; and yet the emotion, the feeling of the friendship remains, and remains unaltered. If the stuff of our thoughts were to alter as the materials of our body alter, the continuity of such an emotion would be impossible. Of course it is difficult to see how, divested of the body, our perceptions can continue; but almost the only thing we are really conscious of is our own identity, our sharp separation from the mass of phenomena that are not ourselves. And, if an emotion can survive the transmutation of the entire frame, may it not also survive the dissolution of that frame?"

"Could it be thus?" I said. "A ray of light falls through a chink in a shutter; through the ray, as we watch it, floats an infinite array of tiny motes, and it is through the striking of the light upon them that we are aware of the light; but they are never the same. Yet the ray has a seeming identity, though even the very ripples of light that cause it are themselves ever changing, ever renewed. Could not the soul be such a ray, illuminating the atoms that pass through it, and itself a perpetual motion, a constant renewal?"

But the day warned us to descend. The shadows grew longer, and a great pale light of sunset began to gather in the West. We came slowly down through the pastures, till we joined the familiar road again. And at last we parted, in that wistful silence that falls upon the mood when two spirits have achieved a certain nearness of thought, have drawn as close as the strange fence of identity allows. But as I went home, I stood for a moment at the edge of a pleasant grove, an outlying pleasaunce of a great house on the verge of the town. The trees grew straight and tall within it, and all the underwood was full of spring flowers and green ground-plants, expanding to light and warmth; the sky was all full of light, dying away to a calm and liquid green, the colour of peace. Here I encountered another friend, a retiring man of letters, who lives apart from the world in dreams of his own. He is a bright-eyed, eager creature, tall and shadowy, who has but a slight hold upon the world. We talked for a few moments of trivial things, till a chance question of mine drew from him a sad statement of his own health. He had been lately, he said, to a physician, and had been warned that he was in a somewhat precarious condition. I tried to comfort him, but he shook his head; and though he tried to speak lightly and cheerfully, I could see that there was a shadow of doom upon him.

As I turned to go, he held up his hand, "Listen to the birds!" he said. We were silent, and could hear the clear flute-like notes of thrushes hidden in the tall trees, and the soft cooing of a dove. "That gives one," he said, "some sense of the happiness which one cannot capture for oneself!" He smiled mournfully, and in a moment I saw his light figure receding among the trees. What a world it is for sorrow! My friend was going, bearing the burden of a lonely grief, which I could not lighten for him; and yet the whole scene was full of so sweet a content, the birds full of hope and delight, the flowers and leaves glad to feel themselves alive. What was one to make of it all? Where to turn for light? What conceivable benefit could result from thus perpetually desiring to know, and perpetually being baffled?

Yet, after all, to-day has been one of those rare days, like the gold sifted from the *débris* of the mine, which has had for me, by some subtle alchemy of the spirit, the permanent quality which is often denied to more stirring incidents and livelier experiences. I had seen the mysteries of life and death, of joy and sorrow, sharply and sadly contrasted. I had been one with Nature, with all her ardent ecstasies, her vital impulses and then I had seen too the other side of the picture, a soul confronted with the mystery of death, alone in the shapeless gloom; the very cries and stirrings and joyful dreams of Nature bringing no help, but only deepening the shadow.

And there came too the thought of how little such easy speculations as we had indulged in on the grassy mound, thoughts which seemed so radiant with beauty and mystery, how little they could sustain or comfort the sad spirit which had entered into the cloud.

So that bright first day of spring shaped itself for me into a day when not only the innocent and beautiful flowers of the world rose into life and sunshine; but a day when sadder thoughts raised their head too, red flowers of suffering, and pale blooms of sadness; and yet these too can be woven into the spirit's coronal, I doubt not, if one can but find heart to do it, and patience for the sorrowful task.

IX

I HAVE just read a story that has moved me strangely, with a helpless bewilderment and a sad anger of mind. When the doors of a factory, in the heart of a northern town, were opened one morning, a workman, going to move a barrel that stood in a corner, saw something crouching behind it that he believed to be a dog or cat. He pushed it with his foot, and a large hare sprang out. I suppose that the poor creature had been probably startled by some dog the evening before, in a field close to the town, had fled in the twilight along the streets, frightened and bewildered, and had slipped into the first place of refuge it had found; had perhaps explored its prison in vain, when the doors were shut, with many dreary perambulations, and had then sunk into an uneasy sleep, with frequent timid awakenings, in the terrifying unfamiliar place.

The man who had disturbed it shouted aloud to the other workmen who were entering; the doors were shut, and the hare was chased by an eager and

excited throng from corner to corner; it fled behind
some planks; the planks were taken up; it made, in
its agony of fear, a great leap over the men who
were bending down to catch it; it rushed into a
corner behind some tanks, from which it was dis-
lodged with a stick. For half an hour the chase
continued, until at last it was headed into a work-
room, where it relinquished hope; it crouched pant-
ing, with its long ears laid back, its pretty brown
eyes wide open, as though wondering desperately
what it had done to deserve such usage; until it was
despatched with a shower of blows, and the limp,
bleeding body handed over to its original discoverer.

Not a soul there had a single thought of pity for
the creature; they went back to work pleased, excited, amused. It was a good story to tell for a
week, and the man who had struck the last blows
became a little hero for his deftness. The old savage instinct for prey had swept fiercely up from the
bottom of these rough hearts—hearts capable, too,
of tenderness and grief, of compassion for suffering, gentle with women and children. It seems to
be impossible to blame them, and such blame would
have been looked upon as silly and misplaced senti-
ment. Probably not even an offer of money, far
in excess of the market value of the dead body, if
the hare could be caught unharmed, would have prevailed at the moment over the instinct for blood.

There are many hares in the world, no doubt, and *nous sommes tous condamnés*. But that the power which could call into being so harmless, pretty, and delicately organised a creature does not care or is unable to protect it better, is a strange mystery. It cannot be supposed that the hare's innocent life deserved such chastisement; and it is difficult to believe that suffering, helplessly endured at one point of the creation, can be remedial at another. Yet one cannot bear to think that the extremity of terror and pain, thus borne by a sensitive creature, either comes of neglect, or of cruel purpose, or is merely wasted. And yet the chase and the slaughter of the unhappy thing cannot be anything but debasing to those who took part in it. And at the same time, to be angry and sorry over so wretched an episode seems like trying to be wiser than the mind that made us. What single gleam of brightness is it possible to extract from the pitiful little story? Only this: that there *must* lie some tender secret, not only behind what seems a deed of unnecessary cruelty, but in the implanting in us of the instinct to grieve with a miserable indignation over a thing we cannot cure, and even in the withholding from us any hope that might hint at the solution of the mystery.

But the thought of the seemly fur stained and bedabbled, the bright hazel eyes troubled with the

fear of death, the silky ears, in which rang the hor-
rid din of pursuit, rises before me as I write, and
casts me back into the sad mood, that makes one
feel that the closer that one gazes into the sorrowful texture of the world, the more glad we may well
be to depart.

X

I HAVE had my imagination deeply thrilled lately
by reading about the discovery in America of the
bones of a fossil animal called the *Diplodocus*. I
hardly know what the word is derived from, but it
might possibly mean an animal which *takes twice as
much,* of nourishment, perhaps, or room; either
twice as much as is good for it, or twice as much as
any other animal. In either case it seems a felicit-
ous description. The creature was a reptile, a
gigantic toad or lizard that lived, it is calculated,
about three million years ago. It was in Canada
that this particular creature lived. The earth was
then a far hotter place than now; a terrible, steaming swamp, full of rank and luxuriant vegetation,
gigantic palms, ferns as big as trees. The diplodocus was upwards of a hundred feet long, a vast
inert creature, with a tough black hide. In spite of
its enormous bulk its brain was only the size of a

pigeon's egg, so that its mental processes must have been of the simplest. It had a big mouth full of rudimentary teeth, of no use to masticate its food, but just sufficing to crop the luxuriant juicy vegetable stalks on which it lived, and of which it ate in the course of the day as much as a small hay-rick would contain. The poisonous swamps in which it crept can seldom have seen the light of day; perpetual and appalling torrents of rain must have raged there, steaming and dripping through the dim and monstrous forests, with their fallen day, varied by long periods of fiery tropical sunshine. In this hot gloom the diplodocus trailed itself about, eating, eating; living a century or so; loving, as far as a brain the size of a pigeon's egg can love, and no doubt with a maternal tenderness for its loathly offspring. It had but few foes, though, in the course of endless generations, there sprang up a carnivorous race of creatures which seem to have found the diplodocus tender eating. The particular diplodocus of which I speak probably died of old age in the act of drinking, and was engulfed in a pool of the great, curdling, reedy river that ran lazily through the forest. The imagination sickens before the thought of the speedy putrefaction of such a beast under such conditions; but this process over, the creature's bones lay deep in the pool.

Another feature of the earth at that date must

have been the vast volcanic agencies at work; whole continents were at intervals submerged or uplifted. In this case the whole of the forest country, where the diplodocus lay, was submerged beneath the sea, and sank to a depth of several leagues; for, in the course of countless ages, sea-ooze, to a depth of at least three miles, was deposited over the forest, preserving the trunks and even the very sprays of the tropical vegetation. Who would suppose that the secret history of this great beast would ever be revealed, as it lay century after century beneath the sea-floor? But another convulsion took place, and a huge ridge of country, forming the rocky backbone of North and South America, was thrust up again by a volcanic convulsion, so that the diplodocus now lay a mile above the sea, with a vast pile of downs over his head which became a huge range of snow mountains. Then the rain and the sun began their work; and the whole of the immense bed of uplifted ocean-silt, now become chalk, was carried eastward by mighty rivers, forming the whole continent of North America, between these mountains and the eastern sea. At last the tropic forest was revealed again, a wide tract of petrified tree-trunks and fossil wood. And then out of an excavation, made where one of the last patches of the chalk still lay in a rift of the hills, where the old river-pool had been into which the great beast had sunk, was dug the neckbone of the creature. Curiosity was aroused by the sight of this fragment of an unknown animal, and bit by bit the great bones came to light; some portions were missing, but further search revealed the remains of three other specimens of the great lizard, and a complete skeleton was put together.

The mind positively reels before the story that is here revealed; we, who are feebly accustomed to regard the course of recorded history as the crucial and critical period of the life of the world, must be sobered by the reflection that the whole of the known history of the human race is not the thousandth, nor the ten-thousandth part of the history of the planet. What does this vast and incredible panorama mean to us? What is it all about? This ghastly force at work, dealing with life and death on so incredible a scale, and yet guarding its secret so close? The diplodocus, I imagine, seldom indulged in reveries as to how it came to be there; it awoke to life; its business was to crawl about in the hot gloom, to eat, and drink, and sleep, to propagate its kind; and not the least amazing part of the history is that at length should have arisen a race of creatures, human beings, that should be able to reconstruct, however faintly, by investigation, imagination, and deduction, a picture of the dead life of the world. It is this capacity for arriving at

what has been, for tracing out the huge mystery of
the work of God, that appears to me the most wonderful thing of all. And yet we seem no nearer to
the solution of the secret; we come into the world
with this incredible gift of placing ourselves, so
to speak, on the side of the Creator, of surveying
his work; and yet we cannot guess what is in his
heart; the stern and majestic eyes of nature behold
us stonily, permitting us to make question, to explore, to investigate, but withholding the secret.
And in the light of those inscrutable eyes, how
weak and arrogant appear our dogmatic systems
of religion, that would profess to define and read
the very purposes of God; our dearest conceptions
of morality, our pathetic principles, pale and fade
before these gigantic indications of mysterious, indifferent energy.

Yet even here, I think, the golden thread gleams
out in the darkness; for slight and frail as our so-
called knowledge, our beliefs, appear, before that
awful, accumulated testimony of the past, yet the
latest development is none the less the instant guiding of God; it is all as much a gift from him as the
blind impulses of the great lizard in the dark forest;
and again there emerges the mighty thought, the
only thought that can give us the peace we seek,
that we are all in his hand, that nothing is forgotten, nothing is small or great in his sight; and that

each of our frail, trembling spirits has its place in the prodigious scheme, as much as the vast and fiery globe of the sun on the one hand, and, on the other, the smallest atom of dust that welters deep beneath the sea.   All that is, exists; indestructible, august, divine, capable of endless rearrangement, infinite modifications, but undeniably there.

This truth, however dimly apprehended, however fitfully followed, ought to give us a certain confidence, a certain patience.   In careless moods we may neglect it; in days of grief and pain we may feel that it cannot help us; but it is the truth; and the more we can make it our own, the deeper that we can set it in our trivial spirits, the better are we prepared to learn the lesson which the deepest instinct of our nature bids us believe, that the Father is trying to teach us, or is at least willing that we should learn if we can.

XI

How strange it is that sometimes the smallest and commonest incident, that has befallen one a hundred times before, will suddenly open the door into that shapeless land of fruitless speculation; the land on to which, I think, the Star Wormwood fell.

burning it up and making it bitter; the land in which we most of us sometimes have to wander, and always alone.

It was such a trifling thing after all. I was bicycling very pleasantly down a country road to-day, when one of those small pungent beetles, a tiny thing, in black plate-armour, for all the world like a minute torpedo, sailed straight into my eye. The eyelid, quicker even than my own thought, shut itself down, but too late. The little fellow was engulphed in what Walt Whitman would call the liquid rims. These small, hard creatures are tenacious of life, and they have, moreover, the power of exuding a noxious secretion—an acrid oil, with a strong scent, and even taste, of saffron. It was all over in a moment. I rubbed my eye, and I suppose crushed him to death; but I could not get him out, and I had no companion to extract him; the result was that my eye was painful and inflamed for an hour or two, till the tiny, black, flattened corpse worked its way out for itself.

Now, that is not a very marvellous incident; but it set me wondering. In the first place, what a horrible experience for the creature; in a moment, as he sailed joyfully along, saying, "Aha," perhaps, like the war-horse among the trumpets, on the scented summer breeze, with the sun warm on his mail, to find himself stuck fast in a hot and oozy crevice, and presently to be crushed to death. His little taste of the pleasant world so soon over, and for me an agreeable hour spoilt, so far as I could see, to no particular purpose.

Now, one is inclined to believe that such an incident is what we call fortuitous; but the only hope we have in the world is to believe that things do not happen by chance. One believes, or tries to believe, that the Father of all has room in his mind for the smallest of his creatures; that not a sparrow, as Christ said, falls to the ground without his tender care. Theologians tell us that death entered into the world by sin; but it is not consistent to believe that, whereas both men and animals suffer and die, the sufferings and death of men are caused by their sins, or by the sins of their ancestors, while animals suffer and die without sin being the cause. Surely the cause must be the same for all the creation? And still less is it possible to believe that the suffering and death of creatures is caused by the sin of man, because they suffered and died for thousands of centuries before man came upon the scene.

If God is omnipotent and all-loving, we are bound to believe that suffering and death are sent by him deliberately, and not cruelly. One single instance, however minute, that established the reverse, would vitiate the whole theory; and if so, then

we are the sport of a power that is sometimes
kind and sometimes malignant. An insupportable
thought!

Is it possible to conceive that the law of sin
works in the lower creation, and that they, too, are
punished, or even wisely corrected, for sinning
against such light as they have? Had the little
beetle that sailed across my path acted in such a
way that he had deserved his fate? Or was his
death meant to make him a better, a larger-minded
beetle? I cannot bring myself to believe that.
Perhaps a philosophical theologian would say that
creation was all one, and that suffering at one point
was remedial at some other point. I am not in a
position to deny the possibility of that, but I am
equally unable to affirm that it is so. There is no
evidence which would lead me to think it. It only
seems to me necessary to affirm it, in order to confirm the axiom that God is omnipotent and all-
loving. Much in nature and in human life would
seem to be at variance with that.

It may be said that one is making too much of a
minute incident; but such incidents are of hourly
occurrence all the world over; and the only possible
method for arriving at truth is the scientific method
of cumulative evidence. The beetle was small, indeed, and infinitely unimportant in the scheme of
things. But he was all in all to himself. The

world only existed so far as he was concerned through his tiny consciousness.

The old-fashioned religious philosophers held that man was the crown and centre of creation, and that God was mainly preoccupied with man's destiny. They maintained that all creatures were given us for our use and enjoyment. The enjoyment that I derived from the beetle, in this case, was not conspicuous. But I suppose that such cheerful optimists would say that the beetle was sent to give me a little lesson in patience, to teach me not to think so much about myself. But, as a matter of fact, the little pain I suffered made me think more of myself than I had previously been doing; it turned me for the time from a bland and hedonistic philosopher into a petulant pessimist, because it seemed that no one was the better for the incident; certainly, if life is worth having at all, the beetle was no better off, and in my own case I could trace no moral improvement. I had been harmlessly enough employed in getting air and exercise in the middle of hard work. It was no vicious enjoyment that was temporarily suspended.

Again, there are people who would say that to indulge in such reveries is morbid; that one must take the rough with the smooth, and not trouble about beetles or inflamed eyes. But if one is haunted by the hopeless desire to search out the

causes of things, such arguments do not assist one.
Such people would say, "Oh, you must take a
larger or wider view of it all, and not strain at
gnats!" But the essence of God's omnipotence
is, that while he can take the infinitely wide view of
all created things, he can also take, I would fain
believe, the infinitely just and minute point of view,
and see the case from the standpoint of the smallest
of his creatures!

What, then, is my solution? That is the melancholy part if it; I am not prepared to offer one. I
am met on every side by hopeless difficulties. I am
tempted to think that God is not at all what we
imagine him to be; that our conceptions of bene-
volence and justice and love are not necessarily true
of him at all. That he is not in the least like our
conceptions of him; that he has no particular tenderness about suffering, no particular care for animal life. Nature would seem to prove that at every
turn; and yet, if it be true, it leaves me struggling
in a sad abyss of thought; it substitutes for our
grave, beautiful, and hopeful conceptions of God
a kind of black mystery which, I confess, lies very
heavy on the heart, and seems to make effort vain.

And thus I fall back again upon faith and hope.
I know that I wish all things well, that I desire
with all my heart that everything that breathes and
moves should be happy and joyful; and I cannot

believe in my heart that it is different with God. And thus I rest in the trust that there is somewhere, far-off, a beauty and a joy in suffering; and that, perhaps, death itself is a fair and a desirable thing.

As I rode to-day in the summer sun, far-off, through the haze, I could see the huge Cathedral towers and portals looming up over the trees. Even so might be the gate of death! As we fare upon our pilgrimage, that shadowy doorway waits, silent and sombre, to receive us. That gate, the gate of death, seems to me, as in strength and health I sweep along the pleasant road of life, a terrible, an appalling place. But shall I feel so, when indeed I tread the threshold, and see the dark arches, the mysterious windows to left and right? It may prove a cool and secure haven of beauty and refreshment, rich in memory, echoing with melodious song. The poor beetle knows about it now, whatever it is; he is wise with the eternal wisdom of all that have entered in, leaving behind them the frail and delicate tabernacle, in which the spirit dwelt, and which is so soon to moulder into dust.

XII

THERE is a big farmyard close to the house where I am staying just now; it is a constant pleasure, as

I pass that way, to stop and watch the manners and customs of the beasts and birds that inhabit it; I am ashamed to think how much time I spend in hanging over a gate, to watch the little dramas of the byre. I am not sure that pigs are an altogether satisfactory subject of contemplation. They always seem to me like a fallen race that has seen better days. They are able, intellectual, inquisitive creatures. When they are driven from place to place, they are not gentle or meek, like cows and sheep, who follow the line of least resistance. The pig is suspicious and cautious; he is sure that there is some uncomfortable plot on foot, not wholly for his good, which he must try to thwart if he can. Then, too, he never seems quite at home in his deplorably filthy surroundings; he looks at you, up to the knees in ooze, out of his little eyes, as if he would live in a more cleanly way, if he were permitted. Pigs always remind me of the mariners of Homer, who were transformed by Circe; there is a dreadful humanity about them, as if they were trying to endure their base conditions philosophically, waiting for their release.

But cows bring a deep tranquillity into the spirit; their glossy skins, their fragrant breath, their contented ease, their mild gaze, their Epicurean rumination tend to restore the balance of the mind, and make one feel that vegetarianism must be a

5

desirable thing.   There is the dignity of innocence about the cow, and I often wish that she did not bear so poor a name, a word so unsuitable for poetry; it is lamentable that one has to take refuge in the archaism of *kine,* when the thing itself is so gentle and pleasant.

But the true joy of the farm-yard is, undoubtedly, in the domestic fowls.   It is long since I was frightened of turkeys; but I confess that there is still something awe-inspiring about an old turkey-cock, with a proud and angry eye, holding his breath till his wattles are blue and swollen, with his fan extended, like a galleon in full sail, his wings held stiffly down, strutting a few rapid steps, and then slowly revolving, like a king in royal robes. There is something tremendous about his supremacy, his almost intolerable pride and glory.

And then we come to cocks and hens.   The farm-yard cock is an incredibly grotesque creature. His furious eye, his blood-red crest, make him look as if he were seeking whom he might devour.   But he is the most craven of creatures.   In spite of his air of just anger, he has no dignity whatever.   To hear him raise his voice, you would think that he was challenging the whole world to combat.   He screams defiance, and when he has done, he looks round with an air of satisfaction.   " There! that is what you have to expect if you interfere with me!"

he seems to say. But an alarm is given; the poultry seek refuge in a hurried flight. Where is the champion? You would expect to see him guarding the rear, menacing his pursuer; but no, he has headed the flight, he is far away, leading the van with a desperate intentness.

This morning I was watching the behaviour of a party of fowls, who were sitting together on a dusty ledge above the road, sheltering from the wind. I do not know whether they meant to be as humorous as they were, but I can hardly think they were not amused at each other. They stood and lay very close together, with fierce glances, and quick, jerky motions of the head. Now and then one, tired of inaction, raised a deliberate claw, bowed its head, scratched with incredible rapidity, shook its tumbled feathers, and looked round with angry self-consciousness, as though to say: "I will ask any one to think me absurd at his peril." Now and then one of them kicked diligently at the soil, and then, turning round, scrutinised the place intently, and picked delicately at some minute object. One examined the neck of her neighbour with a fixed stare, and then pecked the spot sharply. One settled down on the dust, and gave a few vigorous strokes with her legs to make herself more comfortable. Occasionally they all crooned and wailed together, and at the passing of a cart all stood up

defiantly, as if intending to hold their fort at all
hazards.   Presently a woman came out of a house-
door opposite, at which the whole party ran furi-
ously and breathlessly across the road, as if their
lives depended upon arriving in time.   There was
not a gesture or a motion that was not admirably
conceived, intensely dramatic.

Again, what is more delightfully absurd than to
see a hen find a large morsel which she cannot deal
with at one gulp?   She has no sense of diplomacy
or cunning; her friends, attracted by her motions,
close in about her; she picks up the treasured provender, she runs, bewildered with anxiety, till she
has distanced her pursuers; she puts the object down
and takes a couple of desperate pecks; but her kin
are at her heels; another flight follows, another wild
attempt; for half an hour the same tactics are pursued.   At last she is at bay; she makes one prodigious effort, and gets the treasure down with
a convulsive swallow; you see her neck bulge with
the moving object; while she looks at her baffled
companions with an air of meek triumph.

Ducks, too, afford many simple joys to the con-
templative mind.   A slow procession of white
ducks, walking delicately, with heads lifted high
and timid eyes, in a long line, has the air of an
ecclesiastical procession.   The singers go before,
the minstrels follow after.   There is something

liturgical, too, in the way in which, as if by a pre-concerted signal, they all cry out together, standing in a group, with a burst of hoarse cheering, cut off suddenly by an intolerable silence. The arrival of ducks upon the scene, when the fowls are fed, is an impressive sight. They stamp wildly over the pasture, falling, stumbling, rising again, arrive on the scene with a desperate intentness, and eat as though they had not seen food for months.

The pleasure of these farm-yard sights is two-fold. It is partly the sense of grave, unconscious importance about the whole business, serious lives lived with such whole-hearted zeal. There is no sense of divided endeavour; the discovery of food is the one thing in the world, and the sense of re-pletion is also the sense of virtue. But there is something pathetic, too, about the taming to our own ends of these forest beasts, these woodland birds; they are so unconscious of the sad reasons for which we desire their company, so unsuspicious, so serene! Instead of learning by the sorrowful ex-perience of generations what our dark purposes are, they become more and more fraternal, more and more dependent. And yet how little we really know what their thoughts are. They are so unin-telligent in some regions, so subtly wise in others. We cannot share our thoughts with them; we can-not explain anything to them. We can sympathise

with them in their troubles, but cannot convey our
sympathy to them. There is a little bantam hen
here, a great pet, who comes up to the front door
with the other bantams to be fed. She has been
suffering for some time from an obscure illness.
She arrives with the others, full of excitement, and
begins to pick at the grain thrown them; but the
effort soon exhausts her; she goes sadly apart, and
sits with dim eye and ruffled plumage, in silent suffering, wondering, perhaps, why she is not as brisk
and joyful as ever, what is the sad thing that has
befallen her. And one can do nothing, express
nothing of the pathetic sorrow that fills one's mind.
But, none the less, one tries to believe, to feel, that
this suffering is not fortuitous, is not wasted—how
could one endure the thought otherwise, if one did
not hope that "the earnest expectation of the
creature waiteth for the manifestation of the sons
of God!"

XIII

I HAVE been reading with much emotion the life
of a great artist. It is a tender, devoted record;
and there is an atmosphere of delicate beauty about
the style. It is as though his wife, who wrote the
book, had gained through the years of companion-
ship, a pale, pure reflection of her husband's simple

and impassioned style, just as the moon's clear, cold
light is drawn from the hot fountains of the sun.
And yet, there is an individuality about the style,
and the reflection is rather of the same nature as the
patient likeness of expression which is to be seen in
the faces of an aged pair, who have travelled in love
and unity down the vale of years together.

In this artist's own writing, which has a pure and
almost childlike *naïveté* of phrasing, there is a glow,
not of rhetoric or language, but of emotion, an almost lover-like attitude towards his friends, which
is yet saved from sentimentality by an obvious
sincerity of feeling. In this he seems to me to be different from the majority of artistic natures and temperaments. It is impossible not to feel, as a rule,
when one is brought into contact with an artistic
temperament, that the basis of it is a kind of hardness, a fanaticism of spirit. There is, of course, in
the artistic temperament, an abundance of sensitiveness which is often mistaken for feeling. But
it is not generally an unselfish devotion, which desires to give, to lavish, to make sacrifices for the
sake of the beloved. It is, after all, impossible to
serve two masters; and in the highly developed
artist, the central passion is the devotion to art, and
sins against art are the cardinal and unpardonable
sins. The artist has an eager thirst for beautiful
impressions, and his deepest concern is how to

translate these impressions into the medium in which he works. Many an artist has desired and craved for love. But even love in the artist is not the end; love only ministers to the sacred fire of art, and is treated by him as a costly and precious fuel, which he is bound to use to feed the central flame. If one examines the records of great artistic careers, this will, I think, be found to be a true principle; and it is, after all, inevitable that it should be so, in the case of a nature which has the absorbing desire for self-expression. Perhaps, it is not always consciously recognised by the artist, but the fact is there; he tends to regard the deepest and highest experiences of life as ministering to the fulness of his nature. I remember hearing a great master of musical art discussing the music of a young man of extraordinary promise; he said: "Yes, it is very beautiful, very pure; he is perfect in technique and expression, as far as it goes; but it is incomplete and undeveloped. What he wants is to fall in love."

A man who is not bound by the noble thraldom of art, who is full of vitality and emotion, but yet without the imperative desire for self-expression, regards life in a different mood. He may be fully as eager to absorb beautiful impressions, he may love the face of the earth, the glories of hill and plain, the sweet dreams of art, the lingering cadences of music; but he takes them as a child takes food, with a direct and eager appetite, without any impulse to dip them in his own personality, or to find an expression for them. The point for him is not how they strike him and affect him, but that they are there. Such a man will perhaps find his deepest experience in the mysteries of human relationship; and he will so desire the happiness of those he loves, that he will lose himself in efforts to remove obstacles, to lighten burdens, to give rather than to receive joy. And this, I think, is probably the reason why so few women, even those possessed of the most sensitive perception and apprehension, achieve the highest triumphs of art; because they cannot so subordinate life to art, because they have a passionate desire for the happiness of others, and find their deepest satisfaction in helping to further it. Who does not know instances of women of high possibilities, who have quietly sacrificed the pursuit of their own accomplishments to the tendance of some brilliant self-absorbed artist? With such love is often mingled a tender compassionateness, as of a mother for a high-spirited and eager child, who throws herself with perfect sympathy into his aims and tastes, while all the time there sits a gentle knowledge in the background of her heart, of the essential unimportance of the things that the child desires so eagerly, and which she yet desires so whole-heartedly for him. Women

who have made such a sacrifice do it with no
feeling that they are resigning the best for the second best, but because they have a knowledge of
mysteries that are even higher than the mysteries
of art; and they have their reward, not in the contemplation of the sacrifice that they have made, but
in having desired and attained something that is
more beautiful still than any dream that the artist
cherishes and follows.

Yet the fact remains that it is useless to preach
to the artist the mystery that there is a higher region
than the region of art.   A man must aim at the best
that he can conceive; and it is not possible to give
men higher motives by removing the lower motives
that they can comprehend.   Such an attempt is like
building without foundations; and those who have
relations with artists should do all they can to encourage them to aim at what they feel to be the
highest.

But on the other hand, it is a duty for the artist to
keep his heart open, if he can, to the higher influences. He must remember, that though the eye can see
certain colours, and the ear hear certain vibrations
of sound, yet there is an infinite scale of colour, and
an infinite gradation of sound, both above and below what the eye and the ear can apprehend, and
that mortal apprehension can only appropriate to
itself but a tiny fragment of the huge gamut.   He

ought to believe that if he is faithful to the best that he can apprehend, a door may be opened to him which may lead him into regions which are at present closed to him. To accept the artistic conscience, the artistic aim, as the highest ideal of which the spirit is capable, is to be a Pharisee in art, to be self-sufficient, arrogant, limited. It is a kind of spiritual pride, a wilful deafness to more remote voices; and it is thus of all sins, the one which the artist, who lives the life of perception, whose mind must, above all things, be open and transparent, should be loth to commit. He should rather keep his inner eye—for the artist is like the great creatures that, in the prophet's vision, stood nearest to the presence, who were full of eyes, without and within—open to the unwonted apparition which may, suddenly, like a meteor of the night, sail across the silent heaven. It may be that, in some moment of fuller perception, he may even have to divorce the sweeter and more subtle mistress in exchange for one who comes in a homelier guise, and take the beggar girl for his queen. But the abnegation will be no sacrifice; rather a richer and livelier hope.

XIV

WE had a charming idyll here to-day. A young husband and wife came to stay with us in all the first flush of married happiness. One realised all day long that other people merely made a pleasant background for their love, and that for each there was but one real figure on the scene. This was borne witness to by a whole armoury of gentle looks, swift glances, silent gestures. They were both full to the brim of a delicate laughter, of over-brimming wonder, of tranquil desire. And we all took part in their gracious happiness. In the evening they sang and played to us, the wife being an accomplished pianist, the husband a fine singer. But though the glory of their art fell in rainbow showers on the audience, it was for each other that they sang and played. We sat in the dim light of a little panelled room, the lamps making a circle of light about the happy pair; seldom have I felt the revelation of personality more. The wife played to us a handful of beautiful things; but I noticed that she could not interpret the sadder and darker strains, into which the shadow and malady of a suffering spirit had passed; but into little tripping minuets full of laughter and light, and into melodies that spoke of a pure passion of sweetness and human delight, her soul passed, till the room felt as though flooded with the warmth of the sun. And he, too, sang with all his might some joyful and brave utterances, with the lusty pride of manhood; and in a gentler love-song too, that seemed to linger in a dream of delight by crystal streams, the sweet passion of the heart rose clear and true. But when he too essayed a song of sorrow and reluctant sadness, there was no spirit in it; it seemed to him, I suppose, so unlike life, and the joy of life,—so fantastic and unreal an outpouring of the heart.

We sat long in the panelled room, till it seemed all alive with soft dreams and radiant shapes, that floated in a golden air. All that was dark and difficult seemed cast out and exorcised. But it was all so sincere and contented a peace that the darker and more sombre shadows had no jealous awakening; for the two were living to each other, not in a selfish seclusion, but as though they gave of their joy in handfuls to the whole world. The raptures of lovers sometimes take them back so far into a kind of unashamed childishness that the spectacle rouses the contempt and even the indignation of world-worn and cynical people. But here it never deviated from dignity and seemliness; it only seemed new and true, and the best gift of God. These two spirits seemed, with hands interwined, to have ascended gladly into the mountain, and to have seen a transfiguration of life; which left them not in a blissful eminence of isolation, but rather, as it were beckoning others upwards, and saying that the road was indeed easy and plain. And so the sweet hour passed, and left a fragrance behind it; whatever might befall, they had tasted of the holy wine of joy; they had blessed the cup, and bidden us too to set our lips to it.

XV

I WAS walking one summer day in the pleasant hilly country near my home. There is a road which I often traverse, partly because it is a very lonely one, partly because it leads out on a high brow or shoulder of the uplands, and commands a wide view of the plain. Moreover, the road is so deeply sunken between steep banks, overgrown with hazels, that one is hardly aware how much one climbs, and the wide clear view at the top always breaks upon the eye with a certain shock of agreeable surprise. A little before the top of the hill a road turns off, leading into a long disused quarry, surrounded by miniature cliffs, full of grassy mounds and broken ground, overgrown with thickets and floored with rough turf. It is a very enchanting place in spring, and indeed at all times of the year; many flowers grow there, and the birds sing securely among the bushes. I have always imagined that the Red Deeps in *The Mill on the Floss* was just such a place, and the scenes described as taking place there have always enacted themselves for me in the quarry. I have always had a fancy too that if there are any fairies hereabouts, which I very much doubt, for I fear that the new villas which begin to be sprinkled about the countryside have scared them all away, they would be found here. I visited the place one moonlight night, and I am sure that the whole dingle was full of a bright alert life which mocked my clumsy eyes and ears. If I could have stolen upon the place unawares, I felt that I might have seen strange businesses go forward, and tiny revels held.

That afternoon, as I drew near, I was displeased to see that my little retreat was being profaned by company. Some brakes were drawn up in the road, and I heard loud voices raised in untuneful mirth. As I came nearer I was much bewildered to divine who the visitors were. They seemed on the point of departing; two of the brakes were full, and into another some men were clambering. As I came close to them I was still more puzzled. The majority of the party were dressed all alike, in rough brown clothes, with soft black felt hats; but in each of the brakes that were tenanted sat a man as well, with a braided cap, in a sort of uniform. Most of the other men were old or elderly; some had white beards or whiskers, almost all were grizzled. They were talking, too, in an odd, inconsequent, chirping

kind of way, not listening to each other; and moreover they were strangely adorned.   Some had their
hats stuck full of flowers, others were wreathed
with leaves. A few had chains of daisies round their
necks.   They seemed as merry and as obedient as
children.   Inside the gate, in the centre of the
quarry, was a still stranger scene.   Here was a
ring of elderly and aged men, their hats wreathed
with garlands, hand-in-hand, executing a slow and
solemn dance in a circle.   One, who seemed the
moving spirit, a small wiry man with a fresh-col-
oured face and a long chin-beard, was leaping high
in the air, singing some rustic song, and dragging
his less active companions round and round.   The
others all entered into the spirit of the dance.   One
very old and feeble man, with a smile on his face,
was executing little clumsy hops, deeply intent on
the performance.   A few others stood round admiring the sport; a little apart was a tall grave
man, talking loudly to himself, with flowers stuck
all over him, who was spinning round and round in
an ecstasy of delight.   Becoming giddy, he took
a few rapid steps to the left, but fell to the ground,
where he lay laughing softly, and moving his hands
in the air. Presently one of the officials said a word
to the leader of the dance; the ring broke up, and
the performers scattered, gathering up little
bundles of leaves and flowers that lay all about in

some confusion, and then trooping out to the brakes. The quarry was deserted. Several of the group waved their hands to me, uttering unintelligible words, and holding out flowers.

I was so much surprised at the odd scene that I asked one of the officials what it all meant. He said politely that it was a picnic party from the Pauper Lunatic Asylum at H——. The mystery was explained. I said: " They seem to be enjoying themselves." " Yes, indeed, sir," he said, " they are like children; they look forward to this all the year; there is no greater punishment than to deprive a man of his outing." He entered the last brake as he said these words, and the carriages moved off, a shrill and aged cheer rising from thin and piping voices on the air.

The whole thing did not strike me as grotesque, but as infinitely pathetic and even beautiful. Here were these old pitiful creatures, so deeply afflicted, condemned most of them to a lifelong seclusion, who were recalling and living over again their childish sports and delights. What dim memories of old spring days, before their sad disabilities had settled upon them, were working in those aged and feeble brains! What pleased me best was the obvious and light-hearted happiness of the whole party, a compensation for days of starved monotony. No party of school-children on a holiday could have been

6

more thoughtlessly, more intently gay.   Here was
a desolate company, one would have thought, of
life's failures, facing one of the saddest and least
hopeful prospects that the world can afford; yet
on this day at least they were full to the brim of
irresponsible and complete happiness and delight,
tasting an enjoyment, it seemed, more vivid than
often falls to my own lot.   In the presence of such
happiness it seemed so useless, so unnecessary to
ask why so heavy a burden was bound on their
backs, because here at all events was a scene of the
purest and most innocent rapture.   I went on my
way full of wonder and even of hope.   I could not
fathom the deep mystery of the failure, the suffering, the weakness that runs across the world like an
ugly crack across the face of a fair building.   But
then how tenderly and wisely does the great Arti-
ficer lend consolation and healing, repairing and
filling so far as he may, the sad fracture; he seems
to know better than we can divine the things that
belong to our peace; so that as I looked across the
purple rolling plain, with all its wooded ridges, its
rich pastures, the smoke going up from a hundred
hamlets, a confidence, a quiet trust seemed to rise
in my mind, filling me with a strange yearning to
know what were the thoughts of the vast Mind that
makes us and sustains us, mingled with a faith in
some large and far-off issue that shall receive and

enfold our little fretful spirits, as the sea receives the troubled leaping streams, to move in slow unison with the wide and secret tides.

XVI

I WENT to-day to see an old friend whom I had not met for ten years. Some time ago he had a bad fall which for a time crippled him, but from which it was hoped he would recover; but he must have received some obscure and deep-seated injury, because, after improving for a time, he began to go backwards, and has now to a great extent lost the use of his limbs. He was formerly a very active man, both intellectually and physically. He had a prosperous business in the country town on the outskirts of which he lives. He was one of those tall, spare men, black-haired and black-eyed, capable of bearing great fatigue, full to the brim of vitality. He was a great reader, fond of music and art; married to a no less cultivated and active wife, but childless. There never was a man who had a keener enjoyment of existence in all its aspects. It used to be a marvel to me to see at how many points a man could touch life, and the almost child-like zest which he threw into everything which he did.

On arriving at the house, a pleasant old-fashioned place with a big shady garden, I was shown into a large book-lined study, and there presently crept and tottered into the room, leaning on two sticks, a figure which I can only say in no respect recalled to me the recollection of my friend. He was bent and wasted, his hair was white; and there was that sunken look about the temples, that tracery of lines about the eyes that tells of constant suffering. But the voice was unaltered, full, resonant, and distinct as ever. He sat down and was silent for a moment. I think that the motion even from one room into another caused him great pain. Then he began to talk; first he told me of the accident, and his journeys in search of health. " But the comfort is," he added, " that the doctors have now decided that they can do no more for me, and I need leave home no more." He told me that he still went to his business every day—and I found that it was prospering greatly—and that though he could not drive, he could get out in a wheeled chair; he said nothing of his sufferings, and presently began to talk of books and politics. Gradually I realised that I was in the company of a thoroughly cheerful man. It was not the cheerfulness that comes of effort, of a determined attempt to be interested in old pursuits, but the abundant and overflowing cheerfulness of a man who has still a firm grasp on life. He argued, he discussed with the same eager liveliness; and his laugh had the careless and good-humoured ring of a man whose mind was entirely content.

His wife soon entered; and we sat for a long time talking. I was keenly moved by the relations between them; she displayed none of that minute attention to his needs, none of that watchful anxiety which I have often thought, tenderly lavished as it is upon invalids, must bring home to them a painful sense of their dependence and helplessness; and he too showed no trace of that fretful exigence which is too often the characteristic of those who cannot assist themselves, and which almost invariably arises in the case of eager and active temperaments thus afflicted, those whose minds range quickly from subject to subject, and who feel their disabilities at every turn. At one moment he wanted his glasses to read something from a book that lay beside him. He asked his wife with a gentle courtesy to find them. They were discovered in his own breast-pocket, into which he could not even put his feeble hand, and he apologised for his stupidity with an affectionate humility which made me feel inclined to tears, especially when I saw the pleasure which the performance of this trifling service obviously caused her. It was just the same, I afterwards noticed, with a young

attendant who waited on him at luncheon, an occasion which revealed to me the full extent of his
helplessness.

I gathered from his wife in the course of the afternoon that though his life was not threatened,
yet that there was no doubt that his helplessness
was increasing. He could still hold a book and
turn the pages; but it was improbable that he could
do so for long, and he was amusing himself by in-
venting a mechanical device for doing this. But
she too talked of the prospect with a quiet tranquillity. She said that he was making arrangements to direct his business from his house, as it
was becoming difficult for him to enter the office.

He himself showed the same unabated cheerfulness during the whole of my visit, and spoke of the
enjoyment it had brought him. There was not the
slightest touch of self-pity about his talk.

I should have admired and wondered at the fortitude of this gallant pair, if I had seen signs of repression and self-conquest about them; if they had
relapsed even momentarily into repining, if they
had shown signs of a faithful determination to
make the best of a bad business. But I could discern no trace of such a mood about either of them.
Whether this kindly and sweet patience has been
acquired, after hard and miserable wrestlings with
despair and wretchedness, I cannot say, but I am in-

clined to think that it is not so. It seems to me
rather to be the display of perfect manliness and
womanliness in the presence of an irreparable
calamity, a wonderful and amazing compensation,
sent quietly from the deepest fortress of Love to
these simple and generous natures, who live in each
other's lives. I tried to picture to myself what my
own thoughts would be if condemned to this sad
condition; I could only foresee a fretful irritability,
a wild anguish, alternating with a torpid stupefaction. " I seem to love the old books better than
ever," my friend had said, smiling softly, in the
course of the afternoon; " I used to read them hur-
riedly and generally in the old days but now I
have time to think over them—to reflect—I never
knew what a pleasure reflection was." I could not
help feeling as he said the words that with me such a
stroke as he has suffered would have dashed the life,
the colour, out of books, and left them faded and
withered husks. Half the charm of books, I have
always thought, is the interplay of the commentary
of life and experience. I ventured to ask him if
this was not the case. " No," he said, " I don't
think it is—I seem more interested in people, in
events, in thoughts than ever; and one gets them
from a purer spring—I don't know if I can explain," he added, " but I think that one sees it all
from a different perspective, in a truer light, when

one's own desires and possibilities are so much more limited." When I said good-bye to him, he smiled at me and hoped that I should repeat my visit. "Don't think of me as unhappy," he added, and his wife, who was standing by him, said, "Indeed you need not;" and the two smiled at each other in a way which made me feel that they were speaking the simple truth, and that they had found an interpretation of life, a serene region to abide in, which I, with all my activities, hopes, fears, businesses, had somehow missed. The pity of it! and yet the beauty of it! As I went away I felt that I had indeed trodden on holy ground, and seen the transfiguration of humanity and pain into something august, tranquil, and divine.

XVII

THERE are certain things in the world that are so praiseworthy that it seems a needless, indeed an almost laughable thing to praise them; such things are love and friendship, food and sleep, spring and summer; such things, too, are the wisest books, the greatest pictures, the noblest cities. But for all that I mean to try and make a little hymn in prose in honour of Oxford, a city I have seen but seldom, and which yet appears to me one of the most beautiful things in the world.

I do not wish to single out particular buildings, but to praise the whole effect of the place, such as it seemed to me on a day of bright sun and cool air, when I wandered hour after hour among the streets, bewildered and almost intoxicated with beauty, feeling as a poor man might who has pinched all his life, and made the most of single coins, and who is brought into the presence of a heap of piled-up gold, and told that it is all his own.

I have seen it said in foolish books that it is a misfortune to Oxford that so many of the buildings have been built out of so perishable a vein of stone. It is indeed a misfortune in one respect, that it tempts men of dull and precise minds to restore and replace buildings of incomparable grace, because their outline is so exquisitely blurred by time and decay. I remember myself, as a child, visiting Oxford, and thinking that some of the buildings were almost shamefully ruinous of aspect; now that I am wiser I know that we have in these battered and fretted palace-fronts a kind of beauty that fills the mind with an almost despairing sense of loveliness, till the heart aches with gratitude, and thrills with the desire to proclaim the glory of the sight aloud.

These black-fronted blistered façades, so threatening, so sombre, yet screening so bright and clear a current of life; with the tender green of budding spring trees, chestnuts full of silvery spires, glossy-leaved creepers clinging, with tiny hands, to cornice and parapet, give surely the sharpest and most delicate sense that it is possible to conceive of the contrast on which the essence of so much beauty depends.   To pass through one of these dark and smoke-stained courts, with every line mellowed and harmonised, as if it had grown up so out of the earth; to find one's self in a sunny pleasaunce, carpeted with velvet turf, and set thick with flowers, makes the spirit sigh with delight.   Nowhere in the world can one see such a thing as those great gate-piers, with a cognisance a-top, with a grille of iron-work between them, all sweetly entwined with some slim vagrant creeper, that gives a glimpse and a hint —no more—of a fairy-land of shelter and fountains within.   I have seen such palaces stand in quiet and stately parks, as old, as majestic, as finely proportioned as the buildings of Oxford; but the very blackness of the city air, and the drifting smoke of the town, gives that added touch of grimness and mystery that the country airs cannot communicate. And even fairer sights are contained within; those panelled, dark-roofed halls, with their array of portraits gravely and intently regarding the stranger; the chapels, with their splendid classical screens and stalls, rich and dim with ancient glass.   The towers, domes, and steeples; and all set not in a mere paradise of lawns and glades, but in the very heart of a city, itself full of quaint and ancient houses, but busy with all the activity of a brisk and prosperous town; thereby again giving the strong and satisfying sense of contrast, the sense of eager and everyday cares and pleasures, side by side with these secluded havens of peace, the courts and cloisters, where men may yet live a life of gentle thought and quiet contemplation, untroubled, nay, even stimulated, by the presence of a bustling life so near at hand, which yet may not intrude upon the older dream.

I do not know whether my taste is entirely trustworthy, but I confess that I find the Italianate and classical buildings of Oxford finer than the Gothic buildings. The Gothic buildings are quainter, perhaps, more picturesque, but there is an air of solemn pomp and sober dignity about the classical buildings that harmonises better with the sense of wealth and grave security that is so characteristic of the place. The Gothic buildings seem a survival, and have thus a more romantic interest, a more poetical kind of association. But the classical porticoes and façades seem to possess a nobler dignity, and to provide a more appropriate setting for modern Oxford; because the spirit of Oxford is more the spirit of the Renaissance than the spirit of the Schoolmen; and personally I prefer that ecclesiasticism should be more of a flavour than a temper; I mean that though I rejoice to think that sober ecclesiastical influences contribute a serious grace to the life of Oxford, yet I am glad to feel that the spirit of the place is liberal rather than ecclesiastical. Such traces as one sees in the chapels of the Oxford Movement, in the shape of paltry stained glass, starved reredoses, modern Gothic woodwork, would be purely deplorable from the artistic point of view, if they did not possess a historical interest. They speak of interrupted development, an attempt to put back the shadow on the dial, to return to a narrower and more rigid tone, to put old wine into new bottles, which betrays a want of confidence in the expansive power of God. I hate with a deep-seated hatred all such attempts to bind and confine the rising tide of thought. I want to see religion vital and not formal, elastic and not cramped by precedent and tradition. And thus I love to see worship enshrined in noble classical buildings, which seem to me to speak of a desire to infuse the intellectual spirit of Greece, the dignified imperialism of Rome into the more timid and secluded ecclesiastical life, making it fuller, larger, more free, more deliberate.

But even apart from the buildings, which are after all but the body of the place, the soul of Oxford, its inner spirit, is what lends it its satisfying

charm. On the one hand, it gives the sense of the
dignity of the intellect; one reflects that here can be
lived lives of stately simplicity, of high enthusiasm,
apart from personal wealth, and yet surrounded by
enough of seemly dignity to give life the charm of
grave order and quiet solemnity. Here are opportunity for peaceful and congenial work, to the sound
of melodious bells, uninterrupted hours, as much
society of a simple kind as a man can desire, and the
whole with a background of exquisite buildings and
rich gardens. And then, too, there is the tide of
youthful life that floods every corner of the place.
It is an endless pleasure to see the troops of slim
and alert young figures, full of enjoyment and life,
with all the best gifts of life, health, work, amusement, society, friendship, lying ready to their hand.
The sense of this beating and thrilling pulse of life
circulating through these sombre and splendid
buildings is what gives the place its inner glow; this
life full of hope, of sensation, of emotion, not yet
shadowed, or disillusioned, or weary, seems to be as
the fire on the altar, throwing up its sharp-darting
tongues of flame, its clouds of fragrant smoke,
giving warmth and significance and a fiery heart to
a sombre shrine.

And so it is that Oxford is in a sort a magnetic
pole for England; a pole not, perhaps, of intellectual energy, or strenuous liberalism, or clamorous

aims, or political ideas; few, perhaps, of the sturdy
forces that make England great, centre there. The
greatness of England is, I suppose, made up by
her breezy, loud-voiced sailors, her lively, plucky
soldiers, her ardent, undefeated merchants, her
tranquil administrators; by the stubborn adven-
turous spirit that makes itself at home everywhere,
and finds it natural to assume responsibilities.
But to Oxford set the currents of what may be
called intellectual emotion, the ideals that may not
make for immediate national greatness, but which,
if delicately and faithfully nurtured, hold out at
least a hope of affecting the intellectual and spiritual life of the world.   There is something about
Oxford which is not in the least typical of England, but typical of the larger brotherhood that is
independent of nationalities; that is akin to the
spirit which in any land and in every age has produced imperishable monuments of the ardent human
soul.   The tribe of Oxford is the tribe from whose
heart sprang the Psalms of David; Homer and
Sophocles, Plato and Virgil, Dante and Goethe are
all of the same divine company.   It may be said
that John Bull, the sturdy angel of England,
turns his back slightingly upon such influences;
that he regards Oxford as an incidental ornament
of his person, like a seal that jingles at his fob.
But all generous and delicate spirits do her a secret

homage, as a place where the seeds of beauty and emotion, of wisdom and understanding, are sown, as in a secret garden. Hearts such as these, even whirling past that celestial city, among her poor suburbs, feel an inexpressible thrill at the sight of her towers and domes, her walls and groves. *Quam dilecta sunt tabernacula*, they will say; and they will breathe a reverent prayer that there may be no leading into captivity and no complaining in her streets.

XVIII

I FOUND myself at dinner the other day next to an old friend, whom I see but seldom; a quiet, laborious, able man, with the charm of perfect modesty and candour, who, moreover, writes a very beautiful and lucid style. I said to him that I conceived it to be my mission, whenever I met him, to enquire what he was writing, and to beg him to write more. He said smilingly that he was very much occupied in his work, which is teaching, and found little time to write; " besides," he said, " I think that one writes too much." He went on to say that though he loved writing well enough when he was in the mood for it, yet that the labour of shaping sentences, and lifting them to their places, was very severe.

I felt myself a little rebuked by this, for I will here confess that writing is the one pleasure and preoccupation of my own life, though I do not publish a half of what I write. It set me wondering whether I did indeed write too much; and so I said to him: "You mean, I suppose, that one gets into the habit of serving up the same ideas over and over again, with a different sauce, perhaps; but still the same ideas?" "Yes," he said, "that is what I mean. When I have written anything that I care about, I feel that I must wait a long time before the cistern fills again."

We went on to talk of other things; but I have since been reflecting whether there is truth in what my friend said. If this view is true of writing, then it is surely the only art that is so hampered. We should never think that an artist worked too much; we might feel that he did not perhaps finish his big pictures sufficiently; but if he did not spare labour in finishing his pictures, we should never find fault with him for doing, say, as Turner did, and making endless studies and sketches, day after day, of all that struck him as being beautiful. We should feel indeed that some of these unconsidered and rapid sketches had a charm and a grace that the more elaborate pictures might miss; and in any case we should feel that the more that he worked, the firmer and easier would become his sweep of

hand, the more deft his power of indicating a large
effect by an economy of resource.   The musician,
too: no one would think of finding fault with him
for working every day at his art; and it is the same
with all craftsmen; the more they worked, the surer
would their touch be.

Now I am inclined to believe that what makes
writing good is not so much the pains taken with
a particular piece of work, the retouching, the cor-
rections, the dear delays.   Still more fruitful than
this labour is the labour spent on work that is never
used, that never sees the light.   Writing is to me
the simplest and best pleasure in the world; the
mere shaping of an idea in words is the occupation
of all others I most love; indeed, to speak frankly,
I plan and arrange all my days that I may secure
a space for writing, not from a sense of duty, but
merely from a sense of delight.   The whole world
teems with subjects and thoughts, sights of beauty
and images of joy and sorrow, that I desire to put
into words; and to forbid myself to write would be
to exercise the strongest self-denial of which I am
capable.   Of course I do not mean that I can always please myself: I have piles of manuscripts
laid aside which fail either in conception or expression, or in both.   But there are a dozen books I
would like to write if I had the time.

To be honest, I do not believe in fretting too

7

much over a piece of writing. Writing, laboriously constructed, painfully ornamented, is often, I think, both laborious and painful to read; there is a sense of strain about it. It is like those uneasy figures that one sees in the carved gargoyles of old churches, crushed and writhing for ever under a sense of weight painfully sustained, or holding a gaping mouth open, for the water-pipe to discharge its contents therethrough. However ingenious these carvings are, they always give a sense of tension and oppression to the mind; and it is the same with laboured writers; my theory of writing rather is that the conception should be as clear as possible, and then that the words should flow like a transparent stream, following as simply as possible the shape and outline of the thought within, like a waterbreak over a boulder in a stream's bed. This, I think, is best attained by infinite practice. If a piece of work seems to be heavy and muddy, let it be thrown aside ungrudgingly; but the attempt, even though it be a failure, makes the next attempt easier.

I do not think that one can write for very long at a time to much purpose; I take the two or three hours when the mind is clearest and freshest, and write as rapidly as I can; this secures, it seems to me, a clearness and a unity which cannot be attained by fretful labour, by poking and pinching at

one's work. One avoids by rapidity and ardour
the dangerous defect of repetition; a big task must
be divided into small sharp episodes to be thus
swiftly treated. The thought of such a writer as
Flaubert lying on his couch or pacing his room, the
racked and tortured medium of his art, spending
hours in selecting the one perfect word for his purpose, is a noble and inspiring picture; but such a
process does not, I fear, always end in producing
the effect at which it aims; it improves the texture
at a minute point; it sacrifices width and freedom.

Together with clearness of conception and resource of vocabulary must come a certain eagerness
of mood. When all three qualities are present, the
result is good work, however rapidly it may be produced. If one of the three is lacking, the work
sticks, hangs, and grates; and thus what I feel that
the word-artist ought to do is to aim at working
on these lines, but to be very strict and severe about
the ultimate selection of his work. If, for instance,
in a big task, a section has been dully and im-
potently written, let him put the manuscript aside,
and think no more of it for a while; let him not
spend labour in attempting to mend bad work;
then, on some later occasion, let him again get his
conception clear, and write the whole section again;
if he loves writing for itself he will not care how
often this process is repeated.

I am speaking here very frankly; and I will own that for myself, when the day has rolled past and when the sacred hour comes, I sit down to write with an appetite, a keen rapture, such as a hungry man may feel when he sits down to a savoury meal. There is a real physical emotion that accompanies the process; and it is a deep and lively distress that I feel when I am living under conditions that do not allow me to exercise my craft, at being compelled to waste the appropriate hours in other occupations.

It may be fairly urged that with this intense impulse to write, I ought to have contrived to make myself into a better writer; and it might be thought that there is something either grotesque or pathetic in so much emotional enjoyment issuing in so slender a performance. But the essence of the happiness is that the joy resides in the doing of the work and not in the giving it to the world; and though I do not pretend not to be fully alive to the delight of having my work praised and appreciated, that is altogether a secondary pleasure which in no way competes with the luxury of expression.

I am not ungrateful for this delight; it may, I know, be withdrawn from me; but meanwhile the world seems to be full to the brim of expressive and significant things. There is a beautiful old story of a saint who saw in a vision a shining figure approaching him, holding in his hand a dark and

cloudy globe. He held it out, and the saint looking attentively upon it, saw that it appeared to represent the earth in miniature; there were the
continents and seas, with clouds sweeping over
them; and, for all that it was so minute, he could
see cities and plains, and little figures moving to
and fro. The angel laid his finger on a part of the
globe, and detached from it a small cluster of
islands, drawing them out of the sea; and the saint
saw that they were peopled by a folk, whom he
knew, in some way that he could not wholly understand, to be dreary and uncomforted. He heard a
voice saying, *"He taketh up the isles as a very small
thing;"* and it darted into his mind that his work
lay with the people of those sad islands; that he was
to go thither, and speak to them a message of hope.

It is a beautiful story; and it has always seemed
to me that the work of the artist is like that. He
is to detach from the great peopled globe what little
portion seems to appeal to him most; and he must
then say what he can to encourage and sustain men,
whatever thoughts of joy and hope come most home
to him in his long and eager pilgrimage.

XIX

WE were talking yesterday about the stage, a
subject in which I am ashamed to confess I take

but a feeble interest, though I fully recognise the appeal of the drama to certain minds, and its possibilities.   One of the party, who had all his life been a great frequenter of theatres, turned to me and said: "After all, there is one play which seems to be always popular, and to affect all audiences, the poor, the middle-class, the cultivated, alike— *Hamlet*."   " Yes," I said, " and I wonder why that is? "   " Well," he said, " it is this, I think: that beneath all its subtleties, all its intellectual force, it has an emotional appeal to every one who has lived in the world; every one sees himself more or less in Hamlet; every one has been in a situation in which he felt that circumstances were too strong for him; and then, too," he added, " there is always a deep and romantic interest about the case of a man who has every possible external advantage, youth, health, wealth, rank, love, ardour, and zest, who is yet utterly miserable, and moves to a dark end under a shadow of doom."

I thought, and think, this a profound and delicate criticism.   There is, of course, a great deal more in *Hamlet;* there is its high poetry, its mournful dwelling upon deep mysteries, its supernatural terrors, its worldly wisdom, its penetrating insight; but these are all accessories to the central thought; the conception is absolutely firm throughout.   The hunted soul of Hamlet, after a pleasant and easy

drifting upon the stream of happy events, finds a
sombre curtain suddenly twitched aside, and is
confronted with a tragedy so dark, a choice so desperate, that the reeling brain staggers, and can
hardly keep its hold upon the events and habits of
life. Day by day the shadow flits beside him;
morning after morning he uncloses his sad eyes
upon a world, which he had found so sweet, and
which he now sees to be so terrible; the insistent horror breeds a whole troop of spectres, so that all the
quiet experiences of life, friendship, love, nature,
art, become big with uneasy speculations and sur-
mises; from the rampart-platform by the sea until
the peal of ordnance is shot off, as the poor bodies
are carried out, every moment brings with it some
shocking or brooding experience. Hamlet is not
strong enough to close his eyes to these things; if
for a moment he attempts this, some tragic thought
plucks at his shoulder, and bids the awakened
sleeper look out into the struggling light. Neither
is he strong enough to face the situation with reso-
lution and courage. He turns and doubles before
the pursuing Fury; he hopes against hope that a
door of escape may be opened. He poisons the air
with gloom and suspicion; he feeds with wilful sadness upon the most melancholy images of death and
despair. And though the great creator of this
mournful labyrinth, this atrocious dilemma, can

involve the sad spirit with an art that thrills all the most delicate fibres of the human spirit, he cannot stammer out even the most faltering solution, the smallest word of comfort or hope. He leaves the problem, where he took it up, in the mighty hands of God.

And thus the play stands as the supreme memorial of the tortured spirit. The sad soul of the prince seems like an orange-banded bee, buzzing against the glass of some closed chamber-window, wondering heavily what is the clear yet palpable medium that keeps it, in spite of all its efforts, from re-entering the sunny paradise of tree and flower, that lies so close at hand, and that is yet unattainable; until one wonders why the supreme Lord of the place cannot put forth a finger, and release the ineffectual spirit from its fruitless pain. As the play gathers and thickens to its crisis, one experiences—and this is surely a test of the highest art— the poignant desire to explain, to reason, to comfort, to relieve; even if one cannot help, one longs at least to utter the yearning of the heart, the intense sympathy that one feels for the multitude of sorrows that oppress this laden spirit; to assuage if only for a moment, by an answering glance of love, the fire that burns in those stricken eyes. And one must bear away from the story not only the intellectual satisfaction, the emotional excitement, but a deep desire to help, as far as a man can, the woes of spirits who, all the world over, are in the grip of these dreary agonies.

And that, after all, is the secret of the art that deals with the presentment of sorrow; with the art that deals with pure beauty the end is plain enough; we may stay our hearts upon it, plunge with gratitude into the pure stream, and recognise it for a sweet and wholesome gift of God; but the art that makes sorrow beautiful, what are we to do with that? We may learn to bear, we may learn to hope that there is, in the mind of God, if we could but read it, a region where both beauty and sadness are one; and meanwhile it may teach us to let our heart go out, in love and pity, to all who are bound upon their pilgrimage in heaviness, and passing uncomforted through the dark valley.

XX

A few weeks ago I was staying with a friend of mine, a clergyman in the country. He told me one evening a very sad story about one of his parishioners. This was a man who had been a clerk in a London Bank, whose eyesight had failed, and who had at last become totally blind. He was, at the time when this calamity fell upon him, about forty

years of age.   The Directors of the Bank gave him
a small pension, and he had a very small income of
his own; he was married, with one son, who was
shortly after taken into the Bank as a clerk.   The
man and his wife came into the parish, and took a
tiny cottage, where they lived very simply and
frugally.   But within a year or two his hearing had
also failed, and he had since become totally deaf.
It is almost appalling to reflect upon the condition
of helplessness to which this double calamity can
reduce a man.   To be cut off from the sights and
sounds of the world, with these two avenues of perception closed, so as to be able to take cognisance of
external things only through scent and touch!   It
would seem to be well-nigh unendurable!   He had
learned to read raised type with his fingers, and had
been presented by some friends with two or three
books of this kind.   His speech was, as is always
the case, affected, but still intelligible.   Only the
simplest facts could be communicated to him, by
means of a set of cards, with words in raised type,
out of which a few sentences could be arranged.
But he and his wife had invented a code of touch,
by means of which she was able to a certain extent,
though of course very inadequately, to communicate with him.   I asked how he employed himself,
and I was told that he wrote a good deal,—curious,
rhapsodical compositions, dwelling much on his own

thoughts and fancies. " He sits," said the Vicar,
" for hours together on a bench in his garden, and
walks about, guided by his wife. His sense of both
smell and touch have become extraordinarily acute;
and, afflicted as he is, I am sure he is not at all an
unhappy man." He produced some of the writings of which he had spoken. They were written
in a big, clear hand. I read them with intense interest. Some of them were recollections of his
childish days, set in a somewhat antique and biblical
phraseology. Some of them were curious reveries,
dwelling much upon the perception of natural
things through scent. He complained, I remember, that life was so much less interesting in winter
because scents were so much less sweet and less
complex than in summer. But the whole of the
writings showed a serene exaltation of mind. There
was not a touch of repining or resignation about
them. He spoke much of the æsthetic pleasure
that he received from an increased power of disen-
tangling the component elements of a scent, such
as came from his garden on a warm summer day.
Some of the writings that were shown me were religious in character, in which the man spoke of a
constant sense of the nearness of God's presence,
and of a strange joy that filled his heart.

On the following day the Vicar suggested that
we should go to see him; we turned out of a lane,

and found a little cottage with a thatched roof, standing in a small orchard, bright with flowers. On a bench we saw the man sitting, entirely unconscious of our presence. He was a tall, strongly-built fellow with a beard, bronzed and healthy in appearance. His eyes were wide open, and, but for a curious fixity of gaze, I should not have suspected that he was blind. His hands were folded on his knee, and he was smiling; once or twice I saw his lips move as if he was talking to himself. " We won't go up to him," said the Vicar, " as it might startle him; we will find his wife." So we went up to the cottage door, and knocked. It was opened to us by a small elderly woman, with a grave, simple look, and a very pleasant smile. The little place was wonderfully clean and neat. The Vicar introduced me, saying that I had been much interested in her husband's writings, and had come to call on him. She smiled briskly, and said that he would be much pleased. We walked down the path; when we were within a few feet of him, he became aware of our presence, and turned his head with a quiet, expectant air. His wife went up to him, took his hand, and seemed to beat on it softly with her fingers; he smiled, and presently raised his hat, as if to greet us, and then took up a little writing-pad which lay beside him, and began to write. A little conversation followed, his wife reading out what he had written, and then interpreting our remarks to him. What struck me most was the absence of egotism in what he wrote. He asked the Vicar one or two questions, and desired to know who I was. I went and sat down beside him; he wrote in his book that it was a pleasure to him to meet a stranger. Might he take the liberty of seeing him in his own way? " He means," said the wife, smiling, " might he put his hand on your face —some people do not like it," she added apologetically, " and he will quite understand if you do not." I said that I was delighted; and the blind man thereupon laid his hand upon my sleeve, and with an incredible deftness and lightness of touch, so that I hardly felt it, passed his finger-tips over my coat and waistcoat, lingered for a moment over my watch-chain, then over my tie and collar, and then very gently over my face and hair; it did not last half a minute, and there was something curiously magnetic in the touch of the slim firm fingers. " Now I see him," he wrote; " please thank him." " It will please him," said the Vicar, " if we ask him to describe you." In a moment, after a few touches of his wife's hand, he smiled, and wrote down a really remarkably accurate picture of my appearance. We then asked him a few questions about himself. " Very well and very happy," he wrote, " full of the love of God "; and then added, " You

will perhaps think that I get tired of doing nothing, but the time is too short for all I want to do."
" It is quite true," said his wife, smiling as she read
it. "He is as pleased as a child with everything,
and every one is so good to him." Presently she
asked him to read aloud to us; and in a voice of
great distinctness, he read a few verses of the Book
of Job from a big volume. The voice was high and
resonant, but varied strangely in pitch. He asked
at the end whether we had heard every word, and
being told that we had, smiled very sweetly and
frankly, like a boy who has performed a task well.
The Vicar suggested that he should come for a turn
with us, at which he visibly brightened, and said he
would like to walk through the village. He took
our arms, walking between us; and with a delicate
courtesy, knowing that we could not communicate
with him, talked himself, very quietly and simply,
almost all the way, partly of what he was convinced we were passing,—guessing, I imagine,
mainly by a sense of smell, and interpreting it all
with astonishing accuracy, though I confess I was
often unable even to detect the scents which guided
him. We walked thus for half an hour, listening
to his quiet talk. Two or three people came up to
us. Each time the Vicar checked him, and he held
out his hand to be shaken; in each case he recognised the person by the mere touch of the hand.

"Mrs. Purvis, is n't it?   Well, you see me in very good company this morning, don't you?   It is so kind of the Vicar and his friend to take me out, and it is pleasant to meet friends in the village."   He seemed to know all about the affairs of the place, and made enquiries after various people.

It was a very strange experience to walk thus with a fellow-creature suffering from these sad limitations, and yet to be conscious of being in the presence of so perfectly contented and cheerful a spirit.   Before we parted, he wrote on his pad that he was working hard.   "I am trying to write a little book; of course I know that I can never see it, but I should like to tell people that it is possible to live a life like mine, and to be full of happiness; that God sends me abundance of joy, so that I can say with truth that I am happier now than ever I was in the old days.   Such peace and joy, with so many to love me; so little that I can do for others, except to speak of the marvellous goodness of God, and of the beautiful thoughts he gives me."   "Yes, he has written some chapters," said the faithful wife; "but he does not want any one to see them till they are done."

I shall never forget the sight of the two as we went away: he stood, smiling and waving his hand, under an apple-tree in full bloom, with the sun shining on the flowers.   It gave me the sense of a pure and simple content such as I have rarely experienced. The beauty and strength of the picture have dwelt with me ever since, showing me that a soul can be thus shut up in what would seem to be so dark a prison, with the windows, through which most of us look upon the world, closed and shuttered; and yet not only not losing the joy of life, but seeming to taste it in fullest measure. If one could but accept thus one's own limitations, viewing them not as sources of pleasure closed, but as opening the door more wide to what remains; the very simplicity and rarity of the perceptions that are left, gaining in depth and quality from their isolation. But beyond all this lies that well-spring of inner joy, which seems to be withheld from so many of us. Is it indeed withheld? Is it conferred upon this poor soul simply as a tender compensation? Can we not by quiet passivity, rather than by resolute effort, learn the secret of it. I believe myself that the source is there in many hearts, but that we visit it too rarely, and forget it in the multitude of little cares and businesses, which seem so important, so absorbing. It is like a hidden treasure, which we go so far abroad to seek, and for which we endure much weariness of wandering; while all the while it is buried in our own garden-ground; we have paced to and fro above it many times, never dreaming that the bright thing lay beneath our feet, and within reach of our forgetful hand.

XXI

IT was a bright day in early spring; large fleecy clouds floated in a blue sky; the wind was cool, but the sun lay hot in sheltered places.

I was spending a few days with an old friend, at a little house he calls his Hermitage, in a Western valley; we had walked out, had passed the bridge, and had stood awhile to see the clear stream flowing, a vein of reflected sapphire, among the green water-meadows; we had climbed up among the beech-woods, through copses full of primroses, to a large heathery hill, where a clump of old pines stood inside an ancient earth-work. The forest lay at our feet, and the doves cooed lazily among the tree-tops; beyond lay the plain, with a long range of smooth downs behind, where the river broadened to the sea-pool, which narrowed again to the little harbour; and, across the clustered house-roofs and the lonely church tower of the port, we could see a glint of the sea.

We sat awhile in silence; then " Come," I said, " I am going to be impertinent! I am in a mood to ask questions, and to have full answers."

8

"And I," said my host placidly, " am always in the mood to answer questions."

I would call my friend a poet, because he is sealed of the tribe, if ever man was; yet he has never written verses to my knowledge. He is a big, burly, quiet man, gentle and meditative of aspect; shy before company, voluble in private. Half-humorous, half melancholy. He has been a man of affairs, prosperous, too, and shrewd. But nothing in his life was ever so poetical as the way in which, to the surprise and even consternation of all his friends, he announced one day, when he was turned of forty, that he had had enough of work, and that he would do no more. Well, he had no one to say him nay; he has but few relations, none in any way dependent on him; he has a modest competence; and, being fond of all leisurely things—books, music, the open air, the country, flowers, and the like—he has no need to fear that his time will be unoccupied.

He looked lazily at me, biting a straw. " Come," said I again, " here is the time for a catechism. I have reason to think you are over forty? "

" Yes," said he, " the more's the pity! "

"And you have given up regular work," I said, " for over a year; and how do you like that? "

" Like it? " he said.   " Well, so much that I can never work again; and what is stranger still is that

I never knew what it was to be really busy till I gave up work. Before, I was often bored; now, the day is never long enough for all I have to do."

" But that is a dreadful confession," I said; " and how do you justify yourself for this miserable indifference to all that is held to be of importance?"

" Listen! " he said, smiling and holding up his hand. There floated up out of the wood the soft crooning of a dove, like the over-brimming of a tide of content. " There's the answer," he added. " How does that dove justify his existence? and yet he has not much on his mind."

" I have no answer ready," I said, " though there is one, I am sure, if you will only give me time; but let that come later: more questions first, and then I will deliver judgment. Now, attend to this seriously," I said. " How do you justify it that you are alone in the world, not mated, not a good husband and father? The dove has not got that on his conscience."

"Ah! " said my friend. " I have often asked myself that. But for many years I had not the time to fall in love; if I had been an idle man it would have been different, and now that I am free—well, I regard it as, on the whole, a wise dispensation. I have no domestic virtues; I am a pretty commonplace person, and I think there is no reason why I should perpetuate my own feeble qualities, bind

my dull qualities up closer with the life of the world.
Besides, I have a theory that the world is made now
very much as it was in the Middle Ages.   There
was but one choice then—a soldier or a monk.
Now, I have no combative blood in me; I hate a
row; I am a monk to the marrow of my bones, and
the monks are the failures from the point of view
of race.   No monk should breed monks; there are
enough of his kind in the hive already."

"You a monk?" said I, laughing.   "Why, you
are nothing of the kind; you are just the sort of man
for an adoring wife and a handful of big children.
I must have a better answer."

"Well, then," said he, rather seriously, "I will
give you a better answer.   There are some people
whose affections are made to run, strong and
straight, in a narrow channel.   The world holds
but one woman for a man of that type, and it is his
business to find her; but there are others, and I am
one, who dribble away their love in a hundred channels—in art, in nature, among friends.   To speak
frankly, I have had a hundred such passions.   I
made friends as a boy, quickly and romantically,
with all kinds of people—some old, some young.
Then I have loved books, and music, and, above all,
the earth and the things of the earth.   To the
wholesome, normal man these things are but an
agreeable background, and the real business of life

lies with wife and child and work. But to me the real things have been the beautiful things—sunrise and sunset, streams and woods, old houses, talk, poetry, pictures, ideas. And I always liked my work, too."

"And you did it well?" I said.

"Oh, yes, well enough," he replied. "I have a clear head, and I am conscientious; and then there was some fun to be got out of it at times. But it was never a part of myself for all that. And the reason why I gave it up was not because I was tired of it, but because I was getting to depend too much upon it. I should very soon have been unable to do without it."

"But what is your programme?" I said, rather urgently. "Don't you want to be of some use in the world? To make other people better and happier, for instance."

"My dear boy," said my companion, with a smile, "do you know that you are talking in a very conventional way? Of course, I desire that people should be better and happier, myself among the number; but how am I to set about it? Most people's idea of being better and happier is to make other people subscribe to make them richer. They want more things to eat and drink and wear; they want success and respectability, to be sidesmen and town councillors, and even Members of Parliament.

Nothing is more hopelessly unimaginative than ordinary people's aims and ideas, and the aims and ideas, too, that are propounded from pulpits. I don't want people to be richer and more prosperous; I want them to be poorer and simpler. Which is the better man, the shepherd there on the down, out all day in the air, seeing a thousand pretty things, or the grocer behind his counter, living in an odour of lard and cheese, bowing and fussing, and drinking spirits in the evening? Of course, a wholesome-minded man may be wholesome-minded everywhere and anywhere; but prosperity, which is the Englishman's idea of righteousness, is a very dangerous thing, and has very little of what is divine about it. If I had stuck to my work, as all my friends advised me, what would have been the result? I should have had more money than I want, and nothing in the world to live for but my work. Of course, I know that I run the risk of being thought indolent and unpractical. If I were a prophet, I should find it easy enough to scold everybody, and find fault with the poor, peaceful world. But as I am not, I can only follow my own line of life, and try to see and love as many as I can of the beautiful things that God flings down all round us. I am not a philanthropist, I suppose; but most of the philanthropists I have known have seemed to me tiresome, self-seeking people, with a taste for trying to take everything out of God's hands. I am an individualist, I imagine. I think that most of us have to find our way, and to find it alone. I do try to help a few quiet people at the right moment; but I believe that every one has his own circle—some larger, some smaller—and that one does little good outside it. If every one would be content with that, the world would be mended in a trice."

"I am glad that you, at least, admit that there is something to be mended," I said.

"Oh, yes," said he, "the general conditions seem to me to want mending; but that, I humbly think, is God's matter, and not mine. The world is slowly broadening and improving, I believe. In these days, when we shoot our enemies and then nurse them, we are coming, I believe, to see even the gigantic absurdity of war; but all that side of it is too big for me. I am no philosopher! What I believe we ought to do is to be patient, kind, and courageous in a corner. Now, I will give you an instance. I had a friend who was a good, hard-working clergyman; a brave, genial, courageous creature; he had a town parish not far from here; he liked his work, and he did it well. He was the friend of all the boys and girls in the parish; he worked a hundred useful, humble institutions. He was nothing of a preacher, and a poor speaker; but something generous, honest, happy seemed to radiate from the man. Of course, they could not let him alone. They offered him a Bishopric. All his friends said he was bound to take it; the poor fellow wrote to me, and said that he dared not refuse a sphere of wider influence, and all that. I wrote and told him my mind—namely, that he was doing a splendid piece of quiet, sober work, and that he had better stick to it. But, of course, he did n't. Well, what is the result? He is worried to death. He has a big house and a big household; he is a welcome guest in country-houses and vicarages; he opens churches, he confirms; he makes endless poor speeches, and preaches weak sermons. His time is all frittered away in directing the elaborate machinery of a diocese; and all his personal work is gone. I don't say he does n't impress people. But his strength lay in his personal work, his work as a neighbour and a friend. He is not a clever man; he never says a suggestive thing—he is not a sower of thoughts, but a simple pastor. Well, I regard it as a huge and lamentable mistake that he should ever have changed his course; and the motive that made him do it was a bad one, only disguised as an angel of light. Instead of being the stoker of the train, he is now a distinguished passenger in a first-class carriage."

"Well," I said, "I admit that there is a good

deal in what you say. But if such a summons comes to a man, is it not more simple-minded to follow it dutifully? Is it not, after all, part of the guiding of God?"

"Ah!" said my host, "that is a hard question, I admit. But a man must look deep into his heart, and face a situation of the kind bravely and simply. He must be quite sure that it is a summons from God, and not a temptation from the world. I admit that it may be the former. But in the case of which I have just spoken, my friend ought to have seen that it was the latter. He was made for the work he was doing; he was obviously not made for the other. And to sum it up, I think that God puts us into the world to live, not necessarily to get influence over other people. If a man is worth anything, the influence comes; and I don't call it living to attend public luncheons, and to write unnecessary letters, because public luncheons are things which need not exist, and are only amusements invented by fussy and idle people. I am not at all against people amusing themselves. But they ought to do it quietly and inexpensively, and not elaborately and noisily. The only thing that is certain is that men must work and eat and sleep and die. Well, I want them to enjoy their work, their food, their rest; and then I should like them to enjoy their leisure hours peacefully and quietly.

I have done as much in my twenty years of business as a man in a well-regulated state ought to do in the whole of his life; and the rest I shall give, God willing, to leisure—not eating my cake in a corner, but in quiet good fellowship, with an eye and an ear for this wonderful and beautiful world." And my companion smiled upon me a large, gentle, engaging smile.

"Yes," I said, "you have answered well, and you have given me plenty to think about. And at all events you have a point of view, and that is a great thing."

"Yes," said he, "a great thing, as long as one is not sure one is right, but ready to learn, and not desirous to teach. That is the mistake. We are children at school—we ought not to forget that; but many of us want to sit in the master's chair, and rap the desk, and cane the other children."

And so our talk wandered to other things; then we were silent for a little, while the birds came home to their roosts, and the trees shivered in the breeze of sunset; till at last the golden glow gathered in the west, and the sun went down in state behind the crimson line of sea.

XXII

I DESIRE to do a very sacred thing to-day: to enunciate a couple of platitudes and attest them.

It is always a solemn moment in life when one can sincerely subscribe to a platitude. Platitudes are the things which people of plain minds shout from the steps of the staircase of life as they ascend; and to discover the truth of a platitude by experience means that you have climbed a step higher.

The first enunciation is, that in this world we most of us do what we like. And the corollary to that is, that we most of us like what we do.

Of course, we must begin by taking for granted that we most of us are obliged to do something. But that granted, it seems to me that it is very rare to find people who do not take a certain pleasure in their work, and even secretly congratulate themselves on doing it with a certain style and efficiency. To find a person who has not some species of pride of this nature is very rare. Other people may not share our opinion of our own work. But even in the case of those whose work is most open to criticism, it is almost invariable to find that they resent criticism, and are very ready to appropriate praise. I had a curiously complete instance of this the other day. In a parish which I often visit, the organ in the church is what is called presided over by the most infamous executant I have ever heard—an elderly man, who seldom plays a single chord correctly, and whose attempts to use the pedals are of the nature of tentative and unsuccessful experiments. His performance has lately caused a considerable amount of indignation in the parish, for a new organ has been placed in the church, of far louder tone than the old instrument, and my friend the organist is hopelessly adrift upon it. The residents in the place have almost made up their minds to send a round-robin to the Vicar to ask that the *pulsator organorum,* the beater of the organ, as old Cathedral statutes term him, may be deposed. The last time I attended service, one of those strangely appropriate verses came up in the course of the Psalms, which make troubled spirits feel that the Psalter does indeed utter a message to faithful individual hearts. *" I have desired that they, even my enemies,"* ran the verse, *" should not triumph over me; for when my foot slipped, they rejoiced greatly against me."* In the course of the verse the unhappy performer executed a perfect fandango on the pedals. I looked guiltily at the senior churchwarden, and saw his mouth twitch.

In the same afternoon I fell in with the organist, in the course of a stroll, and discoursed to him in a tone of gentle condolence about the difficulties of a new instrument. He looked blankly at me, and then said that he supposed that some people might find a change of instrument bewildering, but that for himself he felt equally at home on any instrument. He went on to relate a series of compliments that well-known musicians had paid him, which I felt must either have been imperfectly recollected, or else must have been of a consolatory or even ironical nature. In five minutes, I discovered that my friend was the victim of an abundant vanity, and that he believed that his vocation in life was organ-playing.

Again, I remember that, when I was a schoolmaster, one of my colleagues was a perfect byword for the disorder and noise that prevailed in his form. I happened once to hold a conversation with him on disciplinary difficulties, thinking that he might have the relief of confiding his troubles to a sympathising friend. What was my amazement when I discovered that his view of the situation was, that every one was confronted with the same difficulties as himself, and that he obviously believed that he was rather more successful than most of us in dealing with them tactfully and strictly.

I believe my principle to be of almost universal application; and that if one could see into the heart of the people who are accounted, and rightly accounted, to be gross and conspicuous failures, we should find that they were not free from a certain pleasant vanity about their own qualifications and efficiency. The few people whom I have met who

are apt to despond over their work are generally
people who do it remarkably well, and whose ideal
of efficiency is so high that they criticise severely
in themselves any deviation from their standard.
Moreover, if one goes a little deeper—if, for instance, one cordially re-echoes their own criticisms
upon their work—such criticisms are apt to be
deeply resented.

I will go further, and say that only once in the
course of my life have I found a man who did his
work really well, without any particular pride and
pleasure in it.   To do that implies an extraordinary degree of will-power and self-command.

I do not mean to say that, if any professional
person found himself suddenly placed in the possession of an independent income, greater than he
had ever derived from his professional work, his
pleasure in his work would be sufficient to retain
him in the exercise of it.   We have most of us an
unhappy belief in our power of living a pleasurable
and virtuous life of leisure; and the desire to live
what is called the life of a gentleman, which character has lately been defined as a person who has no
professional occupation, is very strong in the hearts
of most of us.

But, for all that, we most of us enjoy our work;
the mere fact that one gains facility, and improves
from day to day, is a source of sincere pleasure,

however far short of perfection our attempts may
fall, and, generally speaking, our choice of a
profession is mainly dictated by a certain feeling
of aptitude for and interest in what we propose
to undertake.

It is, then, a happy and merciful delusion by
which we are bound. We grow, I think, to love
our work, and we grow, too, to believe in our method
of doing it. We cannot, a great preacher once
said, all delude ourselves into believing that we are
richer, handsomer, braver, more distinguished than
others; but there are few of us who do not cherish a
secret belief that, if only the truth were known, we
should prove to be more interesting than others.

To leave our work for a moment, and to turn to
ordinary social intercourse. I am convinced that
the only thing that can account for the large number of bad talkers in the world is the wide-spread
belief that prevails among individuals as to their
power of contributing interest and amusement to a
circle. One ought to keep this in mind, and bear
faithfully and patiently the stream of tiresome talk
that pours, as from a hose, from the lips of diffuse
and lengthy conversationalists. I once made a terrible mistake. From the mere desire of saying
something agreeable, and finding my choice of
praiseworthy qualities limited I complimented an
elderly, garrulous acquaintance on his geniality, on

an evening when I had writhed uneasily under a
steady downpour of talk. I have bitterly rued my
insincerity. Not only have I received innumerable
invitations from the man whom the Americans
would call my complimentee, but when I am in his
company I see him making heroic attempts to make
his conversations practically continuous. How often
since that day have I sympathised with St. James
in his eloquent description of the deadly and
poisonous power of the tongue! A bore is not, as
is often believed, a merely selfish and uninteresting
person. He is often a man who labours conscien-
tiously and faithfully at an accomplishment, the
exercise of which has become pleasurable to him.
And thus a bore is the hardest of all people to con-
vert, because he is, as a rule, conscious of virtue and
beneficence.

On the whole, it is better not to disturb the
amiable delusions of our fellow-men, unless we are
certain that we can improve them. To break the
spring of happiness in a virtuous bore is a serious
responsibility. It is better, perhaps, both in matters of work and in matters of social life, to encourage our friends to believe in themselves. We
must not, of course, encourage them in vicious and
hurtful enjoyment, and there are, of course, bores
whose tediousness is not only not harmless, but a
positively noxious and injurious quality. There

are bores who have but to lay a finger upon a subject of universal or special interest, to make one
feel that under no circumstances will one ever be
able to allow one's thoughts to dwell on the subject
again; and such a person should be, as far as possible, isolated from human intercourse, like a sufferer from a contagious malady. But this
extremity of noxiousness is rare. And it may be
said that, as a rule, one does more to increase happiness by a due amount of recognition and praise,
even when one is recognising rather the spirit of a
performance than the actual result; and such a
course of action has the additional advantage of
making one into a person who is eagerly welcomed
and sought after in all kinds of society.

XXIII

THE fresh wind blew cheerily as we raced, my
friend and I, across a long stretch of rich fen-land.
The sunlight, falling somewhat dimly through a
golden haze, lay very pleasantly on the large pas-
ture-fields. There are few things more beautiful,
I think, than these great level plains; they give one
a delightful sense of space and repose. The distant lines of trees, the far-off church towers, the
long dykes, the hamlets half-hidden in orchards, the
" sky-space and field-silence," give one a feeling of

quiet rustic life lived on a large and simple scale, which seems the natural life of the world.

Our goal was the remains of an old religious house, now a farm. We were soon at the place; it stood on a very gentle rising-ground, once an island above the fen. Two great columns of the Abbey Church served as gate-posts. The house itself lay a little back from the road, a comfortable cluster of big barns and outhouses, with great walnut trees all about, in the middle of an ancient tract of pasture, full of dimpled excavations, in which the turf grew greener and more compact. The farm-house itself, a large irregular Georgian building covered with rough orange plaster, showed a pleasant tiled roof among the barns, over a garden set with venerable sprawling box-trees. We found a friendly old labourer, full of simple talk, who showed us the orchard, with its mouldering wall of stone, pierced with niches, the line of dry stew-ponds, the refectory, now a great barn, piled high with heaps of grain and straw. We walked through byres tenanted by comfortable pigs routing in the dirt. We hung over a paling to watch the creased and discontented face of an old hog, grunting in shrill anticipation of a meal. Our guide took us to the house, where we found a transept of the church, now used as a brew-house, with the line of the staircase still visible, rising up to a door in the wall that led once to the dormitory, down the steps of which, night after night, the shivering and sleepy monks must have stumbled into their chilly church for prayers. The hall of the house was magnificent with great Norman arches, once the aisle of the nave.

The whole scene had the busy, comfortable air of a place full of patriarchal life, the dignity of a thing existing for use and not for show, of quiet prosperity, of garnered provender and well-fed stock. Though it made no deliberate attempt at beauty, it was full of a seemly and homely charm. The face of the old fellow that led us about, chirping fragments of local tradition, with a mild pride in the fact that strangers cared to come and see the place, wore the contented, weather-beaten look that comes of a life of easy labour spent in the open air. His patched gaiters, the sacking tied round him with a cord to serve as an apron, had the same simple appropriateness. We walked leisurely about, gathering a hundred pretty impressions,—as of the old filbert-trees that fringed the orchard, the wallflowers, which our guide called the blood-warriors, on the ruined coping, a flight of pigeons turning with a sharp clatter in the air. At last he left us to go about his little business; and we, sitting on a broken mounting-block in the sunshine, gazed lazily and contentedly at the scene.

We attempted to picture something of the life
of the Benedictines who built the house.   It must
have been a life of much quiet happiness.   We tried
to see in imagination the quaint clustered fabrics,
the ancient church, the cloister, the barns, the out-
buildings.   The brethren must have suffered much
from cold in winter.   The day divided by services,
the nights broken by prayers; probably the time
was dull enough, but passed quickly, like all lives
full of monotonous engagements.   They were not
particularly ascetic, these Benedictines, and insisted
much on manual labour in the open air.   Probably
at first the monks did their farm-work as well; but
as they grew richer, they employed labourers, and
themselves fell back on simpler and easier garden-
work.   Perhaps some few were truly devotional
spirits, with a fire of prayer and aspiration burning
in their hearts; but the majority would be quiet
men, full of little gossip about possible promotions,
about lands and crops, about wayfarers and ecclesi-
astics who passed that way and were entertained.
Very few, except certain officials like the Cellarer,
who would have to ride to market, ever left the pre-
cincts of the place, but laid their bones in the little
graveyard east of the church.   We make a mistake
in regarding the life and the building as having
been so picturesque, as they now appear after the
long lapse of time.   The church was more vener-

able than the rest; but the refectory, at the time of
the dissolution, cannot have been long built; still,
the old tiled place, with its rough stone walls, must
have always had a quaint and irregular air.

Probably it was as a rule a contented and amiable society. The regular hours, the wholesome
fatigue which the rule entailed, must have tended
to keep the inmates in health and good-humour.
But probably there was much tittle-tattle; and a
disagreeable, jealous, or scheming inmate must
have been able to stir up a good deal of strife in a
society living at such close quarters. One thinks
loosely that it must have resembled the life of a
college at the University; but that is an entire mis-
apprehension; for the idea of a college is liberty
with just enough discipline to hold it together,
while the idea of a monastery was discipline with
just enough liberty to make life tolerable.

Well, it is all over now! the idea of the monastic
life, which was to make a bulwark for quiet-minded
people against the rougher world, is no longer
needed. The work of the monks is done. Yet I
gave an affectionate thought across the ages to the
old inmates of the place, whose bones have mould-
ered into the dust of the yard where we sat. It
seemed half-pleasant, half-pathetic to think of them
as they went about their work, sturdy, cheerful figures, looking out over the wide fen with all its clear

pools and reed-beds, growing old in the familiar
scene, passing from the dormitory to the infirmary,
and from the infirmary to the graveyard, in a sure
and certain hope. They too enjoyed the first
breaking of spring, the return of balmy winds, the
pushing up of the delicate flowers in orchard and
close, with something of the same pleasure that I
experience to-day. The same wonder that I feel,
the same gentle thrill speaking of an unattainable
peace, an unruffled serenity that lies so near me in
the spring sunshine, flashed, no doubt, into those
elder spirits. Perhaps, indeed, their heart went
out to the unborn that should come after them, as
my heart goes out to the dead to-day.

And even the slow change that has dismantled
that busy place, and established it as the quiet farmstead that I see, holds a hope within it. There must
indeed have been a sad time when the buildings
were slipping into decay, and the church stood
ruined and roofless. But how soon the scars are
healed! How calmly nature smiles at the eager
schemes of men, breaks them short, and then sets
herself to harmonise and adorn the ruin, till she
makes it fairer than before, writing her patient lesson of beauty on broken choir and tottering wall,
flinging her tide of fresh life over the rents, and
tenderly drawing back the broken fragments into
her bosom. If we could not learn from her not to

fret or grieve, to gather up what remains, to wait patiently and wisely for our change!

So I reasoned softly to myself in a train of gentle thought, till the plough-horses came clattering in, and the labourers plodded gratefully home; and the sun went down over the flats in a great glory of orange light.

XXIV

I BELIEVE that I was once taken to Rydal Mount as a small boy, led there meekly, no doubt, in a sort of dream; but I retain not the remotest recollection of the place, except of a small flight of stone steps, which struck me as possessing some attractive quality or other. And I have since read, I suppose, a good many descriptions of the place; but on visiting it, as I recently did, I discovered that I had not the least idea of what it was like. And I would here shortly speak of the extraordinary kindness which I received from the present tenants, who are indeed of the hallowed dynasty; it may suffice to say that I could only admire the delicate courtesy which enabled people, who must have done the same thing a hundred times before, to show me the house with as much zest and interest, as if I was the first pilgrim that had ever visited the place.

In the first place, the great simplicity of the

whole struck me.   It is like a little grange or farm.
The rooms are small and low, and of a pleasant
domesticity; it is a place apt for a patriarchal life,
where simple people might live at close quarters
with each other.   The house is hardly visible from
the gate.   You turn out of a steep lane, embowered
by trees, into a little gravel sweep, approaching the
house from the side.   But its position is selected
with admirable art; the ground falls steeply in front
of it, and you look out over a wide valley, at the end
of which Windermere lies, a tract of sapphire blue,
among wooded hills and dark ranges.   Behind, the
ground rises still more steeply, to the rocky, grassy
heights of Nab Scar; and the road leads on to a
high green valley among the hills, a place of un-
utterable peace.

In this warm, sheltered nook, hidden in woods,
with its southerly aspect, the vegetation grows with
an almost tropical luxuriance, so that the general
impression of the place is by no means typically
English.   Laurels and rhododendrons grow in
dense shrubberies; the trees are full of leaf; flowers blossom profusely.   There is a little orchard
beneath the house, and everywhere there is the frag-
grant and pungent smell of sun warmed garden-
walks and box-hedges.   There are little terraces
everywhere, banked up with stone walls built into
the steep ground, where stonecrops grow richly.

One of these leads to a little thatched arbour, where the poet often sat; below it, the ground falls very rapidly, among rocks and copse and fern, so that you look out on to the tree-tops below, and catch a glimpse of the steely waters of the hidden lake of Rydal.

Wordsworth lived there for more than thirty years; and half a century has passed since he died. He was a skilful landscape gardener; and I suppose that in his lifetime, when the walks were being constructed and the place laid out, it must have had a certain air of newness, of interference with the old wild peace of the hillside, which it has since parted with. Now it is all as full of a quiet and settled order, as if it had been thus for ever. One little detail deserves a special mention; just below the house, there is an odd, circular, low, grassy mound, said to be the old meeting-place for the village council, in primitive and patriarchal days,—the Mount, from which the place has its name.

I thought much of the stately, simple, self-absorbed poet, whom somehow one never thinks of as having been young; the lines of Milton haunted me, as I moved about the rooms, the garden-terraces:—

> *"In this mount he appeared; under this tree*
> *Stood visible ; among these pines his voice*
> *I heard ; here with him at this fountain talked."*

The place is all permeated with the thought of him,

his deep and tranquil worship of natural beauty, his love of the kindly earth.

I do not think that Wordsworth is one whose memory evokes a deep personal attachment. I doubt if any figures of bygone days do that, unless there is a certain wistful pathos about them; unless something of compassion, some wish to proffer sympathy or consolation, mingles with one's reverence. I have often, for instance, stayed at a house where Shelley spent a few half-rapturous, half-miserable months. There, meditating about him, striving to reconstruct the picture of his life, one felt that he suffered much and needlessly; one would have wished to shelter, to protect him if it had been possible, or at least to have proffered sympathy to that inconsolable spirit. One's heart goes out to those who suffered long years ago, whose love of the earth, of life, of beauty, was perpetually overshadowed by the pain that comes from realising transitoriness and decay.

But Wordsworth is touched by no such pathos. He was extraordinarily prosperous and equable; he was undeniably self-sufficient. Even the sorrows and bereavements that he had to bear were borne gently and philosophically. He knew exactly what he wanted to do, and did it. Those sturdy, useful legs of his bore him many a pleasant mile. He always had exactly as much money as he needed, in order to live his life as he desired. He chose precisely the abode he preferred; his fame grew slowly and solidly. He became a great personage; he was treated with immense deference and respect. He neither claimed nor desired sympathy; he was as strong and self-reliant as the old yeomen of the hills, of whom he indeed was one; his vocation was poetry, just as their vocation was agriculture; and this vocation he pursued in as business-like and intent a spirit as they pursued their farming.

Wordsworth, indeed, was armed at all points by a strong and simple pride, too strong to be vanity, too simple to be egotism. He is one of the few supremely fortunate men in the history of literature, because he had none of the sensitiveness or indecision that are so often the curse of the artistic temperament. He never had the least misgivings about the usefulness of his life; he wrote because he enjoyed it; he ate and drank, he strolled and talked, with the same enjoyment. He had a perfect balance of physical health. His dreams never left him cold; his exaltations never plunged him into depression. He felt the mysteries of the world with a solemn awe, but he had no uneasy questionings, no remorse, no bewilderment, no fruitless melancholy.

He bore himself with the same homely dignity

in all companies alike; he was never particularly interested in any one; he never had any fear of being thought ridiculous or pompous. His favourite reading was his own poetry; he wished every one to be interested in his work, because he was conscious of its supreme importance. He probably made the mistake of thinking that it was his sense of poetry and beauty that made him simple and tranquil. As a matter of fact, it was the simplicity and tranquillity of his temperament that gave him the power of enjoyment in so large a measure. There is no growth or expansion about his life; he did not learn his serene and impassive attitude through failures and mistakes: it was his all along.

And yet what a fine, pure, noble, gentle life it was! The very thought of him, faring quietly about among his hills and lakes, murmuring his calm verse, in a sober and temperate joy, looking everywhere for the same grave qualities among quiet, homekeeping folk, brings with it a high inspiration. But we tend to think of Wordsworth as a father and a priest, rather than as a brother and a friend. He is a leader and a guide, not a comrade. We must learn that, though he can perhaps turn our heart the right way, towards the right things, we cannot necessarily acquire that pure peace, that solemn serenity, by obeying his precepts, unless we to have something of the same strong calmness of soul. In some moods, far from sustaining and encouraging us, the thought of his equable, impassioned life may only fill us with un-utterable envy. But still to have sat in his homely rooms, to have paced his little terraces, does bring a certain imagined peace into the mind, a noble shame for all that is sordid or mean, a hatred for the conventional aims, the pitiful ambitions of the world.

Alas, that the only sound from the little hill-platform, the embowered walks, should be the dull rolling of wheels—motors, coaches, omnibuses—in the road below! That is the shadow of his great-ness. It is a pitiable thought that one of the fruits of his genius is that it has made his holy retreat fashionable. The villas rise in rows along the edges of the clear lakes, under the craggy fell-sides, where the feathery ashes root among the mimic precipices. A stream of chattering, vacuous, indifferent tour-ists pours listlessly along the road from *table-d'hôte* to *table-d'hôte*. The turbid outflow of the vulgar world seems a profanation of these august haunts. One hopes despairingly that something of the spirit of lonely beauty speaks to these trivial heads and hearts. But is there consolation in this? What would the poet himself have felt if he could have foreseen it all?

I descended the hill-road and crossed the valley

highway; it was full of dust; the vehicles rolled
along, crowded with men smoking cigars and reading newspapers, tired women, children whose idea
of pleasure had been to fill their hands with ferns
and flowers torn from cranny and covert.   I
climbed the little hill opposite the great Scar; its
green towering head, with its feet buried in wood,
the hardy trees straggling up the front wherever
they could get a hold among the grey crags, rose in
sweet grandeur opposite to me.   I threaded tracks
of shimmering fern, out of which the buzzing flies
rose round me; I went by silent, solitary places
where the springs soak out of the moorland, while I
pondered over the bewildering ways of the world.
The life, the ideals of the great poet, set in the
splendid framework of the great hills, seemed so
majestic and admirable a thing.   But the visible
results—the humming of silly strangers round his
sacred solitudes, the contaminating influence of
commercial exploitation—made one fruitlessly and
hopelessly melancholy.

But even so the hills were silent; the sun went
down in a great glory of golden haze among the
shadowy ridges.   The valleys lay out at my feet,
the rolling woodland, the dark fells.   There fell a
mood of strange yearning upon me, a yearning for
the peaceful secret that, as the orange sunset slowly
waned, the great hills seemed to guard and hold.

What was it that was going on there, what solemn
pageant, what sweet mystery, that I could only desire to behold and apprehend? I know not! I
only know that if I could discern it, if I could tell
it, the world would stand to listen; its littleness, its
meanness, would fade in that august light; the
peace of God would go swiftly and secretly abroad.

XXV

I AM travelling just now, and am this week at
Dorchester, in the company of my oldest and best
friend. We like the same things; and I can be
silent if I will, while I can also say anything, however whimsical, that comes in my mind; there are
few things better than that in the world, and I
count the precious hours very gratefully; *appono
lucro.*

Dorsetshire gives me the feeling of being a very
old country. The big downs seem like the bases
of great rocky hills which have through long ages
been smoothed and worn away, softened and mellowed, the rocks, grain by grain, carried downwards
into the flat alluvial meadowlands beneath. In
these rich pastures, all intersected with clear
streams, runnels, and water-courses, full at this season of rich water-plants, the cattle graze peacefully.
The downs have been ploughed and sown up to the

sky-line.   Then there are fine tracts of heather and
pines in places.   And then, too, there is a sense of
old humanity, of ancient wars about the land.
There are great camps and earth-works everywhere, with ramparts and ditches, both British and
Roman.   The wolds from which the sea is visible
are thickly covered with barrows, each holding the
mouldering bones of some forgotten chieftain, laid
to rest, how many centuries ago, with the rude
mourning of a savage clan.   I stood on one of the
highest of these the other day, on a great gorse-clad
headland, and sent my spirit out in quest of the old
warrior that lay below—"Audisne haec, Am-
phiaräe, sub terram condite?"   But there was no
answer from the air; though in my sleep one night
I saw a wild, red-bearded man, in a coat of skins,
with rude gaiters, and a hat of foxes's fur on his
head; he carried a long staff in his hand, pointed
with iron, and looked mutely and sorrowfully upon
me.   Who knows if it was he?

And then of later date are many ruinous strong-
holds, with Cyclopean walls, like the huge shattered
bulk of *Corfe,* upon its green hill, between the
shoulders of great downs.   There are broken ab-
beys, pinnacled church-towers in village after village.   And then, too, in hamlet after hamlet, rise
quaint stone manors, high-gabled, many-mullioned,
in the midst of barns and byres.   One of the sweet-

est places I have seen is *Cerne Abbas.* The road to
it winds gently up among steep downs, a full stream
gliding through flat pastures at the bottom. The
hamlet has a forgotten, wistful air; there are many
houses in ruins. Close to the street rises the church-
tower, of rich and beautiful design, with gurgoyles
and pinnacles, cut out of a soft orange stone and
delicately weathered. At the end of the village
stands a big farm-house, built out of the abbey
ruins, with a fine oriel in one of the granaries. In
a little wilderness of trees, the ground covered with
primroses, stands the exquisite old gatehouse with
mullioned windows. I have had for years a poor
little engraving of the place, and it seemed to greet
me like an old friend. Then, in the pasture above,
you can see the old terraces and mounds of the
monastic garden, where the busy Benedictines
worked day by day; further still, on the side of the
down itself, is cut a very strange and ancient monu-
ment. It is the rude and barbarous figure of a
naked man, sixty yards long, as though moving
northwards, and brandishing a huge knotted club.
It is carved deep into the turf, and is overgrown
with rough grass. No one can even guess at the
antiquity of the figure, but it is probably not less
than three thousand years old. Some say that it
records the death of a monstrous giant of the valley.
The good monks Christianised it, and named it

Augustine. But it seems to be certainly one of the frightful figures of which Cæsar speaks, on which captives were bound with twisted osiers, and burnt to death for a Druidical sacrifice. The thing is grotesque, vile, horrible; the very stones of the place seem soaked with terror, cruelty, and death. Even recently foul and barbarous traditions were practised there, it is said, by villagers, who were Christian only in name. Yet it lay peacefully enough to-day, the shadows of the clouds racing over it, the wind rustling in the grass, with nothing to break the silence but the twitter of birds, the bleat of sleep on the down, and the crying of cocks in the straw-thatched village below.

What a strange fabric of history, memory, and tradition is here unrolled, of old unhappy far-off things! How bewildering to think of the horrible agonies of fear, the helpless, stupefied creatures lying bound there, the smoke sweeping over them and the flames crackling nearer, while their victorious foes laughed and exulted round them, and the priests performed the last hideous rites. And all the while God watched the slow march of days from the silent heaven, and worked out His mysterious purposes! And yet, surveying the quiet valley to-day, it seems as though there were no memory of suffering or sorrow in it at all.

We climbed the down; and there at our feet the world lay like a map, with its fields, woods, hamlets, and church-towers, the great rich plain rolling to the horizon, till it was lost in haze. How infinitely minute and unimportant seemed one's own life, one's own thoughts, the schemes of one tiny moving atom on the broad back of the hills. And yet my own small restless identity is almost the only thing in the world of which I am assured!

There came to me at that moment a thrill of the spirit which comes but rarely; a deep hope, the sense of a secret lying very near, if one could only grasp it; an assurance that we are safe and secure in the hand of God, and a certainty that there is a vast reality behind, veiled from us only by the shadows of fears, ambitions, and desires. And the thought, too, came that all the tiny human beings that move about their tasks in the plain beneath— nay, the animals, the trees, the flowers, every blade of grass, every pebble—each has its place in the great and awful mystery. Then came the sense of the vast fellowship of created things, the tender Fatherhood of the God who made us all. I can hardly put the thought into words; but it was one of those sudden intuitions that seem to lie deeper even than the mind and the soul, a message from the heart of the world, bidding one wait and wonder, rest and be still.

XXVI

I WILL put another little sketch side by side with the last, for the sake of contrast; I think it is hardly possible within the compass of a few days to have seen two scenes of such minute and essential difference.   At *Cerne* I had the tranquil loneliness of the country-side, the silent valley, the long faintly-tinted lines of pasture, space, and stillness; the hamlets nestled among trees in the dingles of the down. To-day I went south along a dusty road; at first there were quiet ancient sights enough, such as the huge grass-grown encampment of *Maiden Castle,* now a space of pasture, but still guarded by vast ramparts and ditches, dug in the chalk, and for a thousand years or more deserted.   The downs, where they faced the sea, were dotted with grassy barrows, air-swept and silent.   We topped the hill, and in a moment there was a change; through the haze we saw the roofs of *Weymouth* laid out like a map before us, with the smoke drifting west from innumerable chimneys; in the harbour, guarded by the slender breakwaters, floated great ironclads, black and sinister bulks; and beyond them frowned the dark front of *Portland.*   Very soon the houses began to close in upon the road,—brick-built, pretentious, bow-windowed villas; then we were in the streets, showing a wholesome antiquity in the broad-windowed mansions of mellow brick, which sprang into life when the honest king George III. made the quiet port fashionable by spending his simple summers there. There was the king's lodging itself, Gloucester House, now embedded in a hotel, with the big pilastered windows of its saloons giving it a faded courtly air. Soon we were by the quays, with black red-funnelled steamers unloading, and all the quaint and pretty bustle of a port. We went out to a promontory guarded by an old stone fort, and watched a red merchant steamer roll merrily in, blowing a loud sea-horn. Then over a low-shouldered ridge, and we were by the great inner roads, full of shipping; we sat for a while by the melancholy wells of an ancient Tudor castle, now crumbling into the sea; and then across the narrow causeway that leads on to *Portland*. On our right rose the *Chesil Bank,* that mysterious mole of orange shingle, which the sea, for some strange purpose of its own, has piled up, century after century, for eighteen miles along the western coast. And then the grim front of *Portland Island* itself loomed out above us. The road ran up steeply among the bluffs, through line upon line of grey-slated houses; to the left, at the top of the cliff, were the sunken lines of the huge fort, with the long slopes of its earthworks, the glacis overgrown with grass, and

the guns peeping from their embrasures; to the
left, dipping to the south, the steep grey crags,
curve after curve. The streets were alive with an
abundance of merry young sailors and soldiers,
brisk, handsome boys, with the quiet air of discipline that converts a country lout into a self-
respecting citizen. An old bronzed sergeant led a
child with one hand, and with the other tried to obey
her shrill directions about whirling a skipping-rope,
so that she might skip beside him; he looked at us
with a half-proud, half-shamefaced smile, calling
down a rebuke for his inattention from the girl.

We wound slowly up the steep roads smothered
in dust; landwards the view was all drowned in a
pale haze, but the steep grey cliffs by *Lulworth*
gleamed with a tinge of gold across the sea.

At the top, one of the dreariest landscapes I
have ever seen met the sight. The island lies, so to
speak, like a stranded whale, the great head and
shoulders northwards to the land. The moment
you surmount the top, the huge, flat side of the
monster is extended before you, shelving to the sea.
Hardly a tree grows there; there is nothing but a
long perspective of fields, divided here and there
by stone walls, with scattered grey houses at intervals. There is not a feature of any kind on which
the eye can rest. In the foreground the earth is all
tunnelled and tumbled; quarries stretched in every

direction, with huge, gaunt, straddling, gallows-like structures emerging, a wheel spinning at the top, and ropes travelling into the abyss; heaps of grey *débris,* interspersed with stunted grass, huge excavations, ugly ravines with a spout of grim stone at the seaward opening, like the burrowings of some huge mole. The placid green slopes of the fort give an impression of secret strength, even grandeur. Otherwise it is but a ragged, splashed aquarelle of grey and green. Over the *débris* appear at a distance the blunt ominous chimneys of the convict prison, which seems to put the finishing touch on the forbidding character of the scene.

To-day the landward view was all veiled in haze, which seemed to shut off the sad island from the world. On a clear day, no doubt, the view must be full of grandeur, the inland downs, edged everywhere with the tall scarped cliffs, headland after headland, with the long, soft line of the *Chesil Bank* below them. But on a day of sea mist, it must be, I felt, one of the saddest and most mournful regions in the world, with no sound but the wail of gulls, and the chafing of the surge below.

XXVII

To-DAY I had a singular pleasure heightened by an intermingled strangeness and even terror—

qualities which bring out the quality of pleasure in
the same way that a bourdon in a pedal-point passage brings out the quality of what a German
would, I think, call the *over-work*. I was at
Canterbury, where the great central tower is
wreathed with scaffolding, and has a dim, blurred
outline from a distance, as though it were being
rapidly shaken to and fro. I found a friendly
and communicable man who offered to take me
over it; we climbed a dizzy little winding stair, with
bright glimpses at intervals, through loopholes, of
sunlight and wheeling birds; then we crept along
the top of a vaulted space with great pockets of
darkness to right and left. Soon we were in the
gallery of the lantern, from which we could see the
little people crawling on the floor beneath, like slow
insects. And then we mounted a short ladder
which took us out of one of the great belfry windows, on to the lowest of the planked galleries.
What a frail and precarious structure it seemed:
the planks bent beneath our feet. And here came
the first exquisite delight—that of being close to the
precipitous face of the tower, of seeing the carved
work which had never been seen close at hand since
its erection except by the jackdaws and pigeons. I
was moved and touched by observing how fine and
delicate all the sculpture was. There were rows
and rows of little heraldic devices, which from be-

low could appear only as tiny fretted points; yet
every petal of rose or *fleur-de-lys* was as scrupu-
lously and cleanly cut as if it had been meant to be
seen close at hand; a waste of power, I suppose;
but what a pretty and delicate waste! and done, I
felt, in faithful days, when the carving was done as
much to delight, if possible, the eye of God, as to
please the eye of man. Higher and higher we went,
till at last we reached the parapet. And then by a
dizzy perpendicular ladder to which I committed
myself in faith, we reached a little platform on the
very top of one of the pinnacles. The vane had
just been fixed, and the stone was splashed with the
oozing solder. And now came the delight of the
huge view all round: the wooded heights, the rolling
hills; old church towers rose from flowering orchards; a mansion peeped through immemorial
trees; and far to the north-east we could see the
white cliff of *Pegwell Bay;* endeared to me through
the beautiful picture by Dyce, where the pale crags
rise from the reefs green with untorn weeds. There
on the horizon I could see shadowy sails on the
steely sea-line.

Near at hand there were the streets, and then
the Close, with its comfortable canonical houses,
in green trim gardens, spread out like a map at
my feet. We looked down on to the tops of tall
elm-trees, and saw the rooks walking and sitting

on the grey-splashed platforms of twigs, that
swayed horribly in the breeze. It was pleasant to
see, as I did, the tiny figure of my reverend host
walking, a dot of black, in his garden beneath, reading in a book. The long grey-leaded roof ran
broad and straight, a hundred feet below. One felt
for a moment as a God might feel, looking on a
corner of his created world, and seeing that it was
good. One seemed to have surmounted the earth,
and to watch the little creeping orbits of men with
a benevolent compassion, perceiving how strait they
were. The large air hissed briskly in the pinnacles,
and roared through the belfry windows beneath.
I cannot describe the eager exhilaration which filled
me; but I guessed that the impulse which bids men
fling themselves from such heights is not a morbid
prepossession, not a physical dizziness, but an in-
temperate and overwhelming joy. It seems at
such a moment so easy to float and swim through
the viewless air, as if one would be borne up on the
wings of angels.

But, alas! the hour warned us to return. On
our way down we disturbed a peevish jackdaw
from her nest; she had dragged up to that intolerable height a pile of boughs that would have made
a dozen nests; she had interwoven for the cup to
hold her eggs a number of strips of purloined can-
vas. There lay the three speckled eggs, the hope

of the race, while the chiding mother stood on a pinnacle hard by, waiting for the intruder to begone.

A strange sense of humiliation and smallness came upon me as we emerged at last into the nave; the people that had seemed so small and insignificant, were, alas! as big and as important as myself; I felt as an exile from the porches of heaven, a fallen spirit.

XXVIII

I AM often baffled when I try to think what prayer is; if our thoughts do indeed lie open before the eyes of the Father, like a little clear globe of water which a man may hold in his hand—and I am sure they do—it certainly seems hardly worth while to put those desires into words. Many good Christians seem to me to conceive of prayers partly as a kind of tribute they are bound to pay, and partly as requests that are almost certain to be refused. With such people religion, then, means the effort which they make to trust a Father who hears prayers, and very seldom answers them. But this does not seem to be a very reasonable attitude.

I confess that liturgical prayer does not very much appeal to me. It does not seem to me to

correspond to any particular need in my mind.   It
seems to me to sacrifice almost all the things that I
mean by prayer—the sustained intention of soul,
the laying of one's own problems before the Father,
the expression of one's hopes for others, the desire
that the sorrows of the world should be lightened.
Of course, a liturgy touches these thoughts at many
points; but the exercise of one's own liberty of aspiration and wonder, the pursuing of a train of
thought, the quiet dwelling upon mysteries, are all
lost if one has to stumble and run in a prescribed
track.   To follow a service with uplifted attention
requires more mental agility than I possess; point
after point is raised, and yet, if one pauses to meditate, to wonder, to aspire, one is lost, and misses the
thread of the service.   I suppose that there is or
ought to be something in the united act of intercession.   But I dislike all public meetings, and think
them a waste of time.   I should make an exception
in favour of the Sacrament, but the rapid disap-
pearance of the majority of a congregation before
the solemn act seems to me to destroy the sense of
unity with singular rapidity.   As to the old theory
that God requires of his followers that they should
unite at intervals in presenting him with a certain
amount of complimentary effusion, I cannot even
approach the idea.   The holiest, simplest, most
benevolent being of whom I can conceive would be

inexpressibly pained and distressed by such an intention on the part of the objects of his care; and to conceive of God as greedy of recognition seems to me to be one of the conceptions which insult the dignity of the soul.

I have heard lately one or two mediæval stories which illustrate what I mean. There is a story of a pious monk, who, worn out by long vigils, fell asleep, as he was saying his prayers before a crucifix. He was awakened by a buffet on the head, and heard a stern voice saying, " Is this an oratory or a dormitory? " I cannot conceive of any story more grotesquely human than the above, or more out of keeping with one's best thoughts about God. Again, there is a story which is told, I think, of one of the first monasteries of the Benedictine order. One of the monks was a lay brother, who had many little menial tasks to fulfil; he was a well-meaning man, but extremely forgetful, and he was often forced to retire from some service in which he was taking part, because he had forgotten to put the vegetables on to boil, or omitted other duties which would lead to the discomfort of the brethren. Another monk, who was fond of more secular occupations, such as wood-carving and garden-work, and not at all attached to habits of prayer, seeing this, thought that he would do the same; and he too used to slip away from a service, in order to return to the business that he loved better. The Prior of the monastery, an anxious, humble man, was at a loss how to act; so he called in a very holy hermit, who lived in a cell hard by, that he might have the benefit of his advice. The hermit came and attended an Office. Presently the lay brother rose from his knees and slipped out. The hermit looked up, followed him with his eyes, and appeared to be greatly moved. But he took no action, and only addressed himself more assiduously to his prayers. Shortly after, the other brother rose and went out. The hermit looked up, and seeing him go, rose too, and followed him to the door, where he fetched him a great blow upon the head that nearly brought him to the ground. Thereupon the stricken man went humbly back to his place and addressed himself to his prayers; and the hermit did the same.

The Office was soon over, and the hermit went to the Prior's room to talk the matter over. The hermit said: " I bore in my mind what you told me, dear Father, and when I saw one of the brethren rise from his prayers, I asked God to show me what I should do; but I saw a wonderful thing; there was a shining figure with our brother, his hand upon the other's sleeve; and this fair comrade, I have no doubt, was an angel of God, that led the brother forth, that he might be about his Father's business. So I prayed the more earnestly. But when our other brother rose, I looked up; and I saw that he had been plucked by the sleeve by a little naked, comely boy, very swarthy of hue, that I saw had no business among our holy prayers; he wore a mocking smile on his face, as though he prevailed in evil. So I rose and followed; and just as they came to the door, I aimed a shrewd blow, for it was told me what to do, at the boy, and struck him on the head, so that he fell to the ground, and presently went to his own place; and then our brother came back to his prayers."

The Prior mused a little over this wonder, and then he said, smiling: "It seemed to me that it was our brother that was smitten." "Very like," said the hermit, "for the two were close together, and I think the boy was whispering in the brother's ear; but give God the glory; for the dear brother will not offend again."

There is an abundance of truth in this wholesome ancient tale; but I will not draw the morals out here. All I will say is that the old theory of prayer, simple and childlike as it is, seems to have a curious vitality even nowadays. It presupposes that the act of prayer is in itself pleasing to God; and that is what I am not satisfied of.

That theory seems to prevail even more strongly in the Roman Church of to-day than in our own. The Roman priest is not a man occupied primarily with pastoral duties; his business is the business of prayer.   To neglect his daily offices is a mortal sin, and when he has said them, his priestly duty is at an end.   This does not seem to me to bear any relation to the theory of prayer as enunciated in the Gospel.   There the practice of constant and secret prayer, of a direct and informal kind, is enjoined upon all followers of Christ; but Our Lord seems to be very hard upon the lengthy and public prayers of the Pharisees, and indeed against all formality in the matter at all.   The only united service that he enjoined upon his followers was the Sacrament of the common meal; and I confess that the saying of formal liturgies in an ornate building seems to me to be a practice which has drifted very far away from the simplicity of individual religion which Christ appears to have aimed at.

My own feeling about prayer is that it should not be relegated to certain seasons, or attended by certain postures, or even couched in definite language; it should rather be a constant uplifting of the heart, a stretching out of the hands to God. I do not think we should ask for definite things that we desire; I am sure that our definite desires, our fears, our plans, our schemes, the hope that visits one a hundred times a day, our cravings for wealth, our success or influence, are as easily read by God, as a man can discern the tiny atoms and filaments

that swim in his crystal globe. But I think we may
ask to be led, to be guided, to be helped; we may
put our anxious little decisions before God; we may
ask for strength to fulfil hard duties; we may put
our desires for others' happiness, our hopes for our
country, our compassion for sorrowing or afflicted
persons, our horror of cruelty and tyranny before
him; and here I believe lies the force of prayer;
that by practising this sense of aspiration in his
presence, we gain a strength to do our own part.
If we abstain from prayer, if we limit our prayers
to our own small desires, we grow, I know, petty
and self-absorbed and feeble. We can leave the
fulfilment of our concrete aims to God; but we
ought to be always stretching out our hands and
opening our hearts to the high and gracious mysteries that lie all about us.

A friend of mine told me that a little Russian
peasant, whom he had visited often in a military
hospital, told him, at their last interview, that he
would tell him a prayer that was always effective,
and had never failed of being answered. "But
you must not use it," he said, "unless you are in a
great difficulty, and there seems no way out." The
prayer which he then repeated was this: "Lord,
remember King David, and all his grace."

I have never tested the efficacy of this prayer, but
I have a thousand times tested the efficacy of sud-

den prayer in moments of difficulty, when confronted with a little temptation, when overwhelmed with irritation, before an anxious interview, before writing a difficult passage. How often has the temptation floated away, the irritation mastered itself, the right word been said, the right sentence written! To do all we are capable of, and then to commit the matter to the hand of the Father, that is the best that we can do.

Of course, I am well aware that there are many who find this kind of help in liturgical prayer; and I am thankful that it is so. But for myself, I can only say that as long as I pursued the customary path, and confined myself to fixed moments of prayer, I gained very little benefit. I do not forego the practice of liturgical attendance even now; for a solemn service, with all the majesty of an old and beautiful building full of countless associations, with all the resources of musical sound and ceremonial movement, does uplift and rejoice the soul. And even with simpler services, there is often something vaguely sustaining and tranquillising in the act. But the deeper secret lies in the fact that prayer is an attitude of soul, and not a ceremony; that it is an individual mystery, and not a piece of venerable pomp. I would have every one adopt his own method in the matter. I would not for an instant discourage those who find that liturgical

usage uplifts them; but neither would I have those
to be discouraged who find that it has no meaning
for them.   The secret lies in the fact that our aim
should be a relation with the Father, a frank and
reverent confidence, a humble waiting upon God.
That the Father loves all his children with an equal
love I doubt not.   But he is nearest to those who
turn to him at every moment, and speak to him with
a quiet trustfulness.   He alone knows why he has
set us in the middle of such a bewildering world,
where joy and sorrow, darkness and light, are so
strangely intermingled; and all that we can do is to
follow wisely and patiently such cases as he gives
us, into the cloudy darkness in which he seems to
dwell.

XXIX

I HEARD read the other morning, in a quiet house-
chapel, a chapter which has always seemed to me
one of the most perfectly beautiful things in the
Bible.   And as it was read, I felt, what is always
a test of the highest kind of beauty, that I had never
known before how perfect it was.   It was the 48th
chapter of Genesis, the blessing of Ephraim and
Manasses.   Jacob, feeble and spent, is lying in the
quiet, tranquil passiveness of old age, with bygone
things passing like dreams before the inner eye of

the spirit—in that mood, I think, when one hardly knows where the imagined begins or the real ends. He is told that his son Joseph is coming, and he strengthens himself for an effort. Joseph enters, and, in a strain of high solemnity, Jacob speaks of the promise made long before on the stone-strewn hills of Bethel, and its fulfilment; but even so he seems to wander in his thought, the recollection of his Rachel comes over him, and he cannot forbear to speak of her: *"And as for me, when I came from Padan, Rachel died by me in the land of Canaan, in the way, and when yet there was but a little way to come unto Ephrath; and I buried her there in the way of Ephrath; the same is Bethlehem."*

Could there be anything more human, more tender than that? The memory of the sad day of loss and mouring, and then the gentle, aged precision about names and places, the details that add nothing, and yet are so natural, so sweet an echo of the old tale, the symbols of the story, that stand for so much and mean so little,—*" the same is Bethlehem."* Who has not heard an old man thus tracing out the particulars of some remote recollected incident, dwelling for the hundredth time on the unimportant detail, the side-issue, so needlessly anxious to avoid confusion, so bent on useless accuracy.

Then, as he wanders thus, he becomes aware of

the two boys, standing in wonder and awe beside him; and even so he cannot at once piece together the facts, but asks, with a sudden curiosity, " *Who are these?* " Then it is explained very gently by the dear son whom he had lost, and who stands for a parable of tranquil wisdom and loyal love. The old man kisses and embraces the boys, and with a full heart says, " *I had not thought to see thy face; and lo, God hath showed me also thy seed.*" And at this Joseph can bear it no more, puts the boys forward, who seem to be clinging shyly to him, and bows himself down with his face to the earth, in a passion of grief and awe.

And then the old man will not bless them as intended, but gives the richer blessing to the younger; with those words which haunt the memory and sink into the heart: " *The angel which redeemed me from all evil, bless the lads.*" And Joseph is moved by what he thinks to be a mistake, and would correct it, so as to give the larger blessing to his first-born. But Jacob refuses. " *I know it, my son, I know it . . . he also shall be great, but truly his younger brother shall be greater than he.*"

And so he adds a further blessing; and even then, at that deep moment, the old man cannot refrain from one flash of pride in his old prowess, and speaks, in his closing words, of the inheritance he won from the Amorite with his sword and bow; and this is all the more human because there is no trace in the records of his ever having done anything of the kind.   He seems to have been always a man of peace.   And so the sweet story remains human to the very end.   I care very little what the critics may have to say on the matter.   They may call it legendary if they will, they may say that it is the work of an Ephraimite scribe, bent on consecrating the Ephraimite supremacy by the aid of tradition. But the incident appears to me to be of a reality, a force, a tenderness, that is above historical criticism. Whatever else may be true, there is a breathing reality in the picture of the old weak patriarch making his last conscious effort; Joseph, that wise and prudent   servant,   whose   activities   have   never clouded his clear natural affections; the boys, the mute and awed actors in the scene, not made to utter any precocious phrases, and yet centring the tenderness of hope and joy upon themselves.   If it is art, it is the perfection of art, which touches the very heart-strings into a passion of sweetness and wonder.

Compare this ancient story with other achievements of the human mind and soul: with Homer, with Virgil, with Shakespeare.   I think they pale beside it, because with no sense of effort or construction, with all the homely air of a simple record, the perfectly natural, the perfectly pathetic, the perfectly beautiful, is here achieved. There is no painting of effects, no dwelling on accessories, no consciousness of beauty; and yet the heart is fed, the imagination touched, the spirit satisfied. For here one has set foot in the very shrine of truth and beauty, and the wise hand that wrote it has just opened the door of the heart, and stands back, claiming no reward, desiring no praise.

XXX

I HAVE often thought that the last chapter of St. John's Gospel is one of the most bewildering and enchanting pieces of literature I know. I suppose Robert Browning must have thought so, because he makes the reading of it, in that odd rich poem, *Bishop Blougram's Apology,* the sign, together with testing a plough, of a man's conversion, from the unreal life of talk and words, to the realities of life; though I have never divined why he used this particular chapter as a symbol; and indeed I hope no one will ever make it clear to me, though I daresay the connection is plain enough.

It is bewildering, because it is a postscript, added, with a singular artlessness, after the Gospel has come to a full close. Perhaps St. John did not even write it, though the pretty childlike conclusion about the world itself not being able to contain the books that might be written about Christ has always seemed to me to be in his spirit, the words of a very simple-minded and aged man. It is enchanting, because it contains two of the most beautiful episodes in the whole of the Gospel History, the charge to St. Peter to feed the lambs and sheep of the fold, where one of the most delicate nuances of language is lost in the English translation, and the appearance of Jesus beside the sea of Galilee. I must not here discuss the story of the charge to St. Peter, though I once heard it read, with exquisite pathos, when an archbishop of Canterbury was being enthroned with all the pomp and circumstance of ecclesiastical ceremony, in such a way that it brought out, by a flash of revelation, the true spirit of the scene we were attending; we were simple Christians, it seemed, assembled only to set a shepherd over a fold, that he might lead a flock in green pastures and by waters of comfort.

But a man must not tell two tales at once, or he loses the savour of both. Let us take the other story.

The dreadful incidents of the Passion are over; the shame, the horror, the humiliation, the disappointment. The hearts of the Apostles must have been sore indeed at the thought that they had deserted their friend and Master. Then followed the mysterious incidents of the Resurrection, about

which I will only say that it is plain from the documents, if they are accepted as a record at all, from
the astonishing change which seems to have passed
over the Apostles, converting their timid faithfulness into a tranquil boldness, that they, at all events,
believed that some incredibly momentous thing had
happened, and that their Master was among them
again, returning through the gates of Death.

They go back, like men wearied of inaction, tired
of agitated thought, to their homely trade.   All
night the boat sways in the quiet tide, but they catch
nothing.   Then, as the morning begins to come
in about the promontories and shores of the lake,
they see the figure of one moving on the bank, who
hails them with a familiar heartiness, as a man
might do who had to provide for unexpected guests,
and had nothing to give them to eat.   I fancy, I
know not whether rightly, that they see in him a
purchaser, and answer sullenly that they have
nothing to sell.   Then follows a direction, which
they obey, to cast the net on the right side of the
boat.   Perhaps they thought the stranger—for it
is clear that as yet they had no suspicion of his
identity—had seen some sign of a moving shoal
which had escaped them.   They secure a great haul
of fish.   Then John has an inkling of the truth;
and I know no words which thrill me more strangely
than the simple expression that bursts from his lips:

It is the Lord! With characteristic impetuosity
Peter leaps into the water, and wades or swims
ashore.

And then comes another of the surprising touches
of the story. As a mother might tenderly provide
a meal for her husband and sons who have been out
all night, they find that their visitant has made and
lit a little fire, and is broiling fish, how obtained one
knows not; then the haul is dragged ashore, the big
shoal leaping in the net; and then follows the simple
invitation and the distribution of the food. It
seems as though that memorable meal, by the shore
of the lake, with the fresh brightness of the morning
breaking all about them must have been partaken
of in silence; one can almost hear the soft crackling
of the fire, and the waves breaking on the shingle.
They dared not ask him who he was: they knew;
and yet, considering that they had only parted
from him a few days before, the narrative implies
that some mysterious change must have passed over
him. Perhaps they were wondering, as we may
wonder, how he was spending those days. He was
seen only in sudden and unexpected glimpses;
where was he living, what was he doing through
those long nights and days in which they saw him
not? I can only say that for me a deep mystery
broods over the record. The glimpses of him, and
even more his absences, seem to me to transcend the

powers of human invention. That these men lived, that they believed they saw the Lord, seems to me the only possible explanation, though I admit to the full the baffling mystery of it all.

And then the scene closes with absolute suddenness; there is no attempt to describe, to amplify, to analyse. There follows the charge to Peter, the strange prophecy of his death, and the still stranger repression of curiosity as to what should be the fate of St. John.

But the whole incident, coming to us as it does out of the hidden ancient world, defying investigation, provoking the deepest wonder, remains as faint and sweet as the incense of the morning, as the cool breeze that played about the weary brows of the sleepless fishermen, and stirred the long ripple of the clear lake.

XXXI

I THINK that there are few verses of the Bible that give one a more sudden and startling thrill than the verse at the beginning of the viiith chapter of the Revelation. *And when he had opened the seventh seal there was silence in heaven about the space of half an hour.* The very simplicity of the words, the homely note of specified time, is in itself deeply impressive. But further, it gives the dim sense of some awful and unseen preparation going forward, a period allowed in which those that stood by, august and majestic as they were, should collect their courage, should make themselves ready with bated breath for some dire pageant.   Up to that moment the vision had followed hard on the opening of each seal.   Upon the opening of the first, had resounded a peal of thunder, and the voice of the first beast had called the awestruck eyes and the failing heart to look upon the sight: *Come and see!* Then the white horse with the crowned conqueror had ridden joyfully forth.   At the opening of the second seal, had sprung forth the red horse, and the rider with the great sword.   When the third was opened, the black horse had gone forth, the rider bearing the balances; and then had followed the strange and naïve charge by the unknown voice, which gives one so strong a sense that the vision was being faithfully recorded rather than originated, the voice that quoted a price for the grain of wheat and barley, and directed the protection of the vineyard and olive-yard.   This homely reference to the simple food of earth keeps the mind intent upon the actual realities and needs of life in the midst of these bewildering sights.   Then at the fourth opening, the pale horse, bestridden by Death, went mournfully abroad.   At the fifth seal, the crowded souls beneath the altar cry out for restlessness; they are clothed in white robes, and bidden to be patient for a while. Then, at the sixth seal, falls the earthquake, the confusion of nature, the dismay of men, before the terror of the anger of God; and the very words *the wrath of the Lamb,* have a marvellous significance; the wrath of the Most Merciful, the wrath of one whose very symbol is that of a blithe and meek innocence. Then the earth is guarded from harm, and the faithful are sealed; and in words of the sublimest pathos, the end of pain and sorrow is proclaimed, and the promise that the redeemed shall be fed and led forth by fountains of living waters. And then, at the very moment of calm and peace, the seventh seal is opened,—and nothing follows! the very angels of heaven seem to stand with closed eyes, compressed lips, and beating heart, waiting for what shall be.

And then at last the visions come crowding before the gaze again—the seven trumpets are sounded, the bitter, burning stars fall, the locusts swarm out from the smoking pit, and death and woe begin their work; till at last the book is delivered to the prophet, and his heart is filled with the sweetness of the truth.

I have no desire to trace the precise significance of these things. I do not wish that these tapestries of wrought mysteries should be suspended upon the walls of history. I do not think that they can be so suspended; nor have I the least hope that these strange sights, so full both of brightness and of horror, should ever be seen by mortal eye. But that a human soul should have lost itself in these august dreams, that the book of visions should have been thus strangely guarded through the ages, and at last, clothed in the sweet cadences of our English tongue, should be read in our ears, till the words are soaked through and through with rich wonder and tender associations—that is, I think, a very wonderful and divine thing. The lives of all men that have an inner eye for beauty are full of such mysteries, and surely there is no one, of those that strive to pierce below the dark experiences of life, who is not aware, as he reckons back the days of his life, of hours when the seals of the book have been opened. It has been so, I know, in my own life. Sometimes, at the rending of the seal, a gracious thing has gone forth, bearing victory and prosperity. Sometimes a dark figure has ridden away, changing the very face of the earth for a season. Sometimes a thunder of dismay has followed, or a vision of sweet peace and comfort; and sometimes one has assuredly known that a seal has been broken, to be followed by a silence in heaven and earth.

And thus these solemn and mournful visions retain a great hold over the mind; it is, with myself, partly the childish associations of wonder and delight. One recurred so eagerly to the book, because, instead of mere thought and argument, earthly events, wars and dynasties, here was a gallery of mysterious pictures, things seen out of the body, scenes of bright colour and monstrous forms, enacted on the stage of heaven. That is entrancing still; but beyond and above these strange forms and pictured fancies, I now discern a deeper mystery of thought; not pure and abstract thought, flashes of insight, comforting grace, kindled desires, but rather that more complex thought that, through a perception of strange forms, a waving robe of scarlet, a pavement bright with jewels, a burning star, a bird of sombre plumage, a dark grove, breathes a subtle insight, like a strain of unearthly music, interpreting the hopes and fears of the heart by haunted glimpses and obscure signs. I do not know in what shadowy region of the soul these things draw near, but it is in a region which is distinct and apart, a region where the dreaming mind projects upon the dark its dimly-woven visions; a region where it is not wise to wander too eagerly and carelessly, but into which one may look warily and intently at seasons, standing upon the dizzy edge of time, and gazing out beyond the flaming ramparts of the world.

XXXII

I saw a strange and moving thing to-day. I
went with a friend to visit a great house in the
neighbourhood. The owner was away, but my
friend enjoyed the right of leisurely access to the
place, and we thought we would take the opportunity of seeing it.

We entered at the lodge, and walked through the
old deer-park with its huge knotted oaks, its wide
expanse of grass. The deer were feeding quietly
in a long herd. The great house itself came in
sight, with its portico and pavilions staring at us, so
it seemed, blankly and seriously, with shuttered
eyes. The whole place unutterably still and deserted, like a house seen in a dream.

There was one particular thing that we came
to visit; we left the house on the left, and turned
through a little iron gate into a thick grove of
trees. We soon became aware that there was open
ground before us, and presently we came to a space
in the heart of the wood, where there was a silent
pool all overgrown with water-lilies; the bushes
grew thickly round the edge. The pool was full of
water-birds, coots, and moor-hens, sailing aimlessly
about, and uttering strange, melancholy cries at
intervals. On the edge of the water stood a small
marble temple, streaked and stained by the weather.

As we approached it, my friend told me something of the builder of the little shrine. He was a former owner of the place, a singular man, who in his later days had lived a very solitary life here. He was a man of wild and wayward impulses, who had drunk deeply in youth of pleasure and excitement. He had married a beautiful young wife, who had died childless in the first year of their marriage, and he had abandoned himself after this event to a despairing seclusion, devoted to art and music. He had filled the great house with fine pictures, he had written a book of poems, and some curious stilted volumes of autobiographical prose; but he had no art of expression, and his books had seemed like a powerless attempt to give utterance to wild and melancholy musings; they were written in a pompous and elaborate style, which divested the thoughts of such charm as they might have possessed.

He had lived thus to a considerable age in a wilful sadness, unloving and unloved. He had cared nothing for the people of the place, entertained no visitors; rambling, a proud solitary figure, about the demesne, or immured for days together in his library. Had the story not been true, it would have appeared like some elaborate fiction.

He built this little temple in memory of the wife whom he had lost, and often visited it, spending

12

hours on hot summer days wandering about the little lake, or sitting silent in the portico. We went up to the building. It was a mere alcove, open to the air. But what arrested my attention was a marble figure of a young man, in a sitting position, lightly clad in a tunic, the neck, arms, and knees bare; one knee was flung over the other, and the chin was propped on an arm, the elbow of which rested on the knee. The face was a wonderful and expressive piece of work. The boy seemed to be staring out, not seeing what he looked upon, but lost in a deep agony of thought. The face was wonderfully pure and beautiful; and the anguish seemed not the anguish of remorse, but the pain of looking upon things both sweet and beautiful, and of yet being unable to take a share in them. The whole figure denoted a listless melancholy. It was the work of a famous French sculptor, who seemed to have worked under close and minute direction; and my friend told me that no less than three statues had been completed before the owner was satisfied.

On the pedestal were sculptured the pathetic words, Οἴμοι μαλ' αὖθις. There was a look of revolt of dumb anger upon the face that lay behind its utter and hopeless sadness. I knew too well, by a swift instinct, what the statue stood for. Here was one, made for life, activity, and joy, who yet found himself baffled, thwarted, shut out from the

paradise that seemed to open all about him; it was
the face of one who had found satiety in pleasure,
and sorrow in the very heart of joy. There was no
taint of grossness or of luxury in the face, but rather
a strength, an intellectual force, a firm lucidity of
thought. I confess that the sight moved me very
strangely. I felt a thrill of the deepest compassion, a desire to do something that might help or
comfort, a yearning wish to aid, to explain, to
cheer. The silence, the stillness, the hopelessness
of the pathetic figure woke in me the intensest desire to give I knew not what—an overwhelming
impulse of pity. It seemed a parable of all the joy
that is so sternly checked, all the hopes made vain,
the promise disappointed, the very death of the soul.
It seemed infinitely pathetic that God should have
made so fair a thing, and then withheld joy. And
it seemed as though I had looked into the very soul
of the unhappy man who had set up so strange and
pathetic an allegory of his sufferings. The boy
seemed as though he would have welcomed death—
anything that brought an end; yet the health and
suppleness of the bright figure held out no hope of
that. It was the very type of unutterable sorrow,
and that not in an outworn body, and reflected in a
face dim with sad experience, but in a perfectly
fresh and strong frame, built for action and life.
I cannot say what remote thoughts, what dark com-

munings, visited me at the sight. I seemed confronted all at once with the deepest sadness of the
world, as though an unerring arrow had pierced my
very heart—an arrow winged by beauty, and shot
on a summer day of sunshine and song.

Is there any faith that is strong enough and deep
enough to overcome such questionings? It seemed
to bring me near to all those pale and hopeless
agonies of the world; all the snapping short of joy,
the confronting of life with death—those dreadful
moments when the heart asks itself, in a kind of
furious horror, " How can it be that I am filled so
full of all the instinct of joy and life, and yet bidden
to suffer and to die? "

The only hope is in an utter and silent resignation; in the belief that, if there is a purpose in the
gift of joy, there is a purpose in the gift of suffering. And as thus, in that calm afternoon, in the
silent wood, by the shining pool, I lifted up my
heart to God to be consoled, I felt a great hope
draw near, as when the vast tide flows landward,
and fills the dry, solitary sand-pools with the leaping brine. " Only wait," said the deep and tender
voice, " only endure, only believe; and a sweetness,
a beauty, a truth beyond your utmost dreams shall
be revealed."

XXXIII

HERE is a story which has much occupied my thoughts lately. A man in middle life, with a widowed sister and her children depending on him, living by professional exertions, is suddenly attacked by a painful, horrible, and fatal complaint. He goes through a terrible operation, and then struggles back to his work again, with the utmost courage and gallantry. Again the complaint returns, and the operation is repeated. After this he returns again to his work, but at last, after enduring untold agonies, he is forced to retire into an invalid life, after a few months of which he died in terrible suffering, and leaves his sister and the children nearly penniless.

The man was a quiet, simple-minded person, fond of his work, fond of his home, conventional and not remarkable except for the simply heroic quality he displayed, smiling and joking up to the moment of the administering of anæsthetics for his operations, and bearing his sufferings with perfect patience and fortitude, never saying an impatient word, grateful for the smallest services.

His sister, a simple, active woman, with much tender affection and considerable shrewdness, finding that the fear of incurring needless expense distressed her brother, devoted herself to the ghastly and terrible task of nursing him through his illnesses. The children behaved with the same straightforward affection and goodness. None of the circle ever complained, ever said a word which would lead one to suppose that they had any feeling of resentment or cowardice. They simply received the blows of fate humbly, resignedly, and cheerfully, and made the best of the situation.

Now, let us look this story in the face, and see if we can derive any hope or comfort from it. In the first place, there was nothing in the man's life which would lead one to suppose that he deserved or needed this special chastening, this crucifixion of the body. He was by instinct humble, laborious, unselfish, and good, all of which qualities came out in his illness. Neither was there anything in the life or character of the sister which seemed to need this stern and severe trial. The household had lived a very quiet, active, useful life, models of good citizens—religious, contented, drawing great happiness from very simple resources.

One's belief in the goodness, the justice, the patience of the Father and Maker of men forbids one to believe that he can ever be wantonly cruel, unjust, or unloving. Yet it is impossible to see the mercy or justice of his actions in this case. And the misery is that, if it could be proved that in one single case, however small, God's goodness had, so to speak, broken down; if there were evidence of neglect or carelessness or indifference, in the case of one single child of his, one single sentient thing that he has created, it would be impossible to believe in his omnipotence any more. Either one would feel that he was unjust and cruel, or that there was some evil power at work in the world which he could not overcome.

For there is nothing remedial in this suffering. The man's useful, gentle life is over, the sister is broken down, unhappy, a second time made desolate; the children's education has suffered, their home is made miserable. The only thing that one can see, that is in any degree a compensation, is the extraordinary kindness displayed by friends, relations, and employers in making things easy for the afflicted household. And then, too, there is the heroic quality of soul displayed by the sufferer himself and his sister—a heroism which is ennobling to think of, and yet humiliating too, because it seems to be so far out of one's own reach.

This is a very dark abyss of the world into which we are looking. The case is an extreme one perhaps, but similar things happen every day, in this sad, and wonderful, and bewildering world. Of course, one may take refuge in a gloomy acquiescence, saying that such things seem to be part of the world as it is made, and we cannot explain them, while we dumbly hope that we may be spared such woes. But that is a dark and despairing attitude, and, for one, I cannot live at all, unless I feel that God is indeed more upon our side than that. I cannot live at all, I say. And yet I must live; I must endure the Will of God in whatever form it is laid upon me—in joy or in pain, in contentment or sick despair. Why am I at one with the Will of God when it gives me strength, and hope, and delight? Why am I so averse to it when it brings me languor, and sorrow, and despair? That I cannot tell; and that is the enigma which has confronted men from generation to generation.

But I still believe that there is a Will of God; and, more than that, I can still believe that a day comes for all of us, however far off it may be, when we shall understand; when these tragedies, that now blacken and darken the very air of Heaven for us, will sink into their places in a scheme so august, so magnificent, so joyful, that we shall laugh for wonder and delight; when we shall think not more sorrowfully over these sufferings, these agonies, than we think now of the sad days in our childhood when we sat with a passion of tears over a broken toy or a dead bird, feeling that we could not be comforted. We smile as we remember such things—we smile at our blindness, our limitations. We smile to reflect at the great range and panorama of the world that has opened upon us since, and of which, in our childish grief, we were so ignorant. Under what conditions the glory will be revealed to us I cannot guess. But I do not doubt that it will be revealed; for we forget sorrow, but we do not forget joy.

XXXIV

I HAVE just come back from hearing a great violinist, who played, with three other professors, in two quartettes, Mozart and Beethoven. I know little of the technicalities of music, but I know that the Mozart was full to me of air and sunlight, and a joy which was not the light-hearted gaiety of earth, but the untainted and unwearying joy of heaven; the Beethoven I do not think I understood, but there was a grave minor movement, with pizzicato passages for the violoncello, which seemed to consecrate and dignify the sorrow of the heart.

But apart from the technical merits of the music —and the performance, indeed, seemed to me to lie as near the thought and the conception as the translation of music into sound can go—the sight of these four big men, serious and grave, as though neither pursuing nor creating pleasure, but as though interpreting and giving expression to some weighty secret, had an inspiring and solemnising effect. The sight of the great violinist himself was full of awe; his big head, the full grey beard which lay over the top of the violin, his calm, set brows, his weary eyes with their heavy lids, had a profound dignity and seriousness; and to see his wonderful hands, not delicate or slender, but full, strong, and muscular, moving neither lingeringly nor hastily, but with a firm and easy deliberation upon the strings, was deeply impressive. It all seemed so easy, so inevitable, so utterly without display, so simple and great. It gave one a sense of mingled fire and quietude, which is the end of art,—one may almost say the end of life; it was no leaping and fitful flame, but a calm and steady glow; not a consuming fire, but like the strength of a mighty furnace;—and then the peace of it! The great man did not stand before us as a performer; he seemed utterly indifferent to praise or applause, and he had rather a grave, pontifical air, as of a priest, divinely called to minister, celebrating a divine mystery, calling down the strength of heaven to earth. Neither was there the least sense of one conferring a favour; he rather appeared to recognise that we were there in the same spirit as himself, the worshippers in some high solemnity, and his own skill not a thing to be shown or gloried in, but a mere ministering of a sacred gift. He seemed, indeed, to be like one who distributed a sacramental meat to an intent throng; not a giver of pleasure, but a channel of secret grace.

From such art as this one comes away not only with a thrill of mortal rapture, but with a real and deep faith in art, having bowed the head before a shrine, and having tasted the food of the spirit. When, at the end of a sweet and profound movement, the player raised his great head and looked round tenderly and gently on the crowd, one felt as though, like Moses, he had struck the rock, and the streams had gushed out, *ut bibat populus.* And there fell an even deeper awe, which seemed to say, "God was in this place . . . and I knew it not." The world of movement, of talk, of work, of conflicting interests, into which one must return, seemed all a fantastic noise, a shadowy striving; the only real thing seemed the presence-chamber from which we had gone out, the chamber in which music had uttered its voice at the bidding of some sacred spell, the voice of an infinite Spirit, the Spirit that had brooded upon the deep, evoking order out of chaos and light out of darkness; with no eager and dusty manœuvrings, no clink and clatter of human toil, but gliding resistlessly and largely upon the world, as the sun by silent degrees detaches himself from the dark rim of the world, and climbs in stately progress into the unclouded heaven.

XXXV

I READ a terrible letter in a newspaper this morning, a letter from a clergyman of high position, finding fault with a manifesto put out by certain other clergymen; the letter had a certain volubility about it, and the writer seemed to me to pull out rather adroitly one or two loose sticks in his opponents' bundle, and to lay them vehemently about their backs. But, alas! the acrimony, the positiveness, the arrogance of it!

I do not know that I admired the manifesto very much myself; it was a timid and half-hearted document, but it was at least sympathetic and tender. The purport of it was to say that, just as historical criticism has shown that some of the Old Testament must be regarded as fabulous, so we must be prepared for a possible loss of certitude in some of the details of the New Testament. It is conceivable, for instance, that without sacrificing the least portion of the essential teaching of Christ, men may come to feel justified in a certain suspension of judgment with regard to some of the miraculous occurrences there related; may even grow to believe that an element of exaggeration is there, that element of exaggeration which is never absent from the writings of any age in which scientific historical methods had no existence. A suspension of judgment, say: because in the absence of any converging historical testimony to the events of the New Testament, it will never be possible either to affirm or to deny historically that the facts took place exactly as related; though, indeed, the probability of their having so occurred may seem to be diminished.

The controversialist, whose letter I read with bewilderment and pain, involved his real belief in ingenious sentences, so that one would think that he accepted the statements of the Old Testament, such as the account of the Creation and the Fall, the speaking of Balaam's Ass, the swallowing of Jonah by the whale, as historical facts. He went on to say that the miraculous element of the New Testament is accredited by the Revelation of God, as though some definite revelation of truth had taken place at some time or other, which all rational men recognised. But the only objective process which has ever taken place is, that at certain Councils of the Church, certain books of Scripture were selected as essential documents, and the previous selection of the Old Testament books was confirmed. But would the controversialist say that these Councils were infallible? It must surely be clear to all rational people that the members of these Councils were merely doing their best, under the conditions that then prevailed, to select the books that seemed to them to contain the truth. It is impossible to believe that if the majority at these Councils had supposed that such an account as the account in Genesis of the Creation was mythological, they would thus have attested its literal truth. It never occurred to them to doubt it, because they did not understand the principle that, while a normal event can be accepted, if it is fairly well confirmed, an abnormal event requires a far greater amount of converging testimony to confirm it.

If only the clergy could realise that what ordinary laymen like myself want is a greater elasticity instead of an irrational certainty! if only instead of feebly trying save the outworks, which are already in the hands of the enemy, they would man the walls of the central fortress! If only they would say plainly that a man could remain a convinced Christian, and yet not be bound to hold to the literal accuracy of the account of miraculous incidents recorded in the Bible, it would be a great relief.

I am myself in the position of thousands of other laymen. I am a sincere Christian; and yet I regard the Old Testament and the New Testament alike as the work of fallible men and of poetical minds. I regard the Old Testament as a noble collection of ancient writings, containing myths, chronicles, fables, poems, and dramas, the value of which consists in the intense faith in a personal God and Father with which it is penetrated.

When I come to the New Testament, I feel myself, in the Gospels, confronted by the most wonderful personality which has ever drawn breath upon

the earth. I am not in a position to affirm or to
deny the exact truth of the miraculous occurrences
there related; but the more conscious I am of the
fallibility, the lack of subtlety, the absence of
trained historical method that the writers display,
the more convinced I am of the essential truth of
the person and teaching of Christ, because he seems
to me a figure so infinitely beyond the intellectual
power of those who described him to have invented
or created.

If the authors of the Gospels had been men of
delicate literary skill, of acute philosophical or
poetical insight, like Plato or Shakespeare, then I
should be far less convinced of the integral truth of
the record. But the words and sayings of Christ,
the ideas which he disseminated, seem to me so infinitely above the highest achievements of the human spirit, that I have no difficulty in confessing,
humbly and reverently, that I am in the presence of
one who seems to me to be above humanity, and not
only of it. If all the miraculous events of the Gospels could be proved never to have occurred, it
would not disturb my faith in Christ for an instant.
But I am content, as it is, to believe in the possibility of so abnormal a personality being surrounded by abnormal events, though I am not in a
position to disentangle the actual truth from the
possibilities of misrepresentation and exaggeration.

Dealing with the rest of the New Testament, I see in the Acts of the Apostles a deeply interesting record of the first ripples of the faith in the world. In the Pauline and other epistles I see the words of fervent primitive Christians, men of real and untutored genius, in which one has amazing instances of the effect produced, on contemporary or nearly contemporary persons, of the same overwhelming personality, the personality of Christ. In the Apocalypse I see a vision of deep poetical force and insight.

But in none of these compositions, though they reveal a glow and fervour of conviction that places them high among the memorials of the human spirit, do I recognise anything which is beyond human possibilities. I observe, indeed, that St. Paul's method of argument is not always perfectly consistent, nor his conclusions absolutely cogent. Such inspiration as they contain they draw from their nearness to and their close apprehension of the dim and awe-inspiring presence of Christ himself.

If, as I say, the Church would concentrate her forces in this inner fortress, the personality of Christ, and quit the debatable ground of historical enquiry, it would be to me and to many an unfeigned relief; but meanwhile, neither scientific critics nor irrational pedants shall invalidate my claim to be of the number of believing Christians.

I claim a Christian liberty of thought, while I acknowledge, with bowed head, my belief in God the Father of men, in a Divine Christ, the Redeemer and Saviour, and in the presence in the hearts of men of a Divine spirit, leading humanity tenderly forward. I can neither affirm nor deny the literal accuracy of Scripture records; I am not in a position to deny the superstructure of definite dogma raised by the tradition of the Church about the central truths of its teaching, but neither can I deny the possibility of an admixture of human error in the fabric. I claim my right to receive the Sacraments of my Church, believing as I do that they invigorate the soul, bring the presence of its Redeemer near, and constitute a bond of Christian unity. But I have no reason to believe that any human pronouncement whatever, the pronouncements of men of science as well as the pronouncements of theologians, are not liable to error. There is indeed no fact in the world except the fact of my own existence of which I am absolutely certain. And thus I can accept no system of religion which is based upon deductions, however subtle, from isolated texts, because I cannot be sure of the infallibility of any form of human expression. Yet, on the other hand, I seem to discern with as much certainty as I can discern anything in this world, where all is so dark, the presence upon earth at a certain date of a personality which commands my homage and allegiance.   And upon this I build my trust.

XXXVI

I WAS staying the other day in a large old country-house.   One morning, my host came to me and said: " I should like to show you a curious thing. We have just discovered a cellar here that seems never to have been visited or used since the house was built, and there is the strangest fungoid growth in it I have ever seen."   He took a big bunch of keys, rang the bell, gave an order for lights to be brought, and we went together to the place.   There were ranges of brick-built, vaulted chambers, through which we passed, pleasant, cool places, with no plaster to conceal the native brick, with great wine-bins on either hand.   It all gave one an inkling of the change in material conditions which must have taken place since they were built; the quantity of wine consumed in eighteenth-century days must have been so enormous, and the difficulty of conveyance so great, that every great householder must have felt like the Rich Fool of the parable, with much goods laid up for many years.   In the corner of one of the great vaults was a low arched door, and my friend explained that some panelling

which had been taken out of an older house, de-
molished to make room for the present mansion, had
been piled up here, and thus the entrance had been
hidden. He unlocked the door, and a strange scent
came out. An abundance of lights were lit, and
we went into the vault. It was the strangest scene
I have ever beheld; the end of the vault seemed like
a great bed, hung with brown velvet curtains,
through the gaps of which were visible what seemed
like white velvet pillows, strange humped conglom-
erations. My friend explained to me that there
had been a bin at the end of the vault, out of the
wood of which these singular fungi had sprouted.
The whole place was uncanny and horrible. The
great velvet curtains swayed in the current of air,
and it seemed as though at any moment some mysterious sleeper might be awakened, might peer
forth from his dark curtains, with a fretful enquiry
as to why he was disturbed.

The scene dwelt in my mind for many days, and
aroused in me a strange train of thought; these dim
vegetable forms, with their rich luxuriance, their
sinister beauty, awoke a curious repugnance in the
mind. They seemed unholy and evil. And yet
it is all part of the life of nature; it is just as natural, just as beautiful to find life at work in this
gloomy and unvisited place, wreathing the bare walls
with these dark, soft fabrics. It was impossible

not to feel that there was a certain joy of life in
these growths, sprouting with such security and
luxuriance in a place so precisely adapted to their
well-being; and yet there was the shadow of death
and darkness about them, to us whose home is the
free air and the sun. It seemed to me to make a
curious parable of the baffling mystery of evil, the
luxuriant growth of sin in the dark soul. I have
always felt that the reason why the mystery of evil
is so baffling is because we so resolutely think of evil
as of something inimical to the nature of God; and
yet evil must derive its vitality from him. The one
thing that it is impossible to believe is that, in a
world ruled by an all-powerful God, anything
should come into existence which is in opposition
to his Will. It is impossible to arrive at any solution of the difficulty, unless we either adopt the belief that God is not all-powerful, and that there is a
real dualism in nature, two powers in eternal opposition; or else realise that evil is in some way a
manifestation of God. If we adopt the first
theory, we may conceive of the stationary tendency
in nature, its inertness, the force that tends to bring
motion to a standstill, as one power, the power of
Death; and we may conceive of all motion and
force as the other power, the quickening spirit, the
power of life. But even here we are met with a
difficulty, for when we try to transfer this dualism

to the region of humanity, we see that in the phenomena of disease we are confronted, not with inertness fighting against motion, but with one kind of
life, which is inimical to human life, fighting with
another kind of life which is favourable to health.
I mean that when a fever or a cancer lays hold of a
human frame, it is nothing but the lodging inside
the body of a bacterial and an infusorial life which
fights against the healthy native life of the human
organism. There must be, I will not say a consciousness, but a sense of triumphant life, in the
cancer which feeds upon the limb, in spite of all
efforts to dislodge it; and it is impossible to me to
believe that the vitality of those parasitical organisms, which prey upon the human frame, is not
derived from the vital impulse of God. We, who
live in the free air and the sun, have a way of thinking and speaking as if the plants and animals which
develop under the same conditions were of a healthy
type, while the organisms which flourish in decay
and darkness, such as the fungi of which I saw so
strange an example, the larvæ which prey on decay-
ing matter, the soft and pallid worm-like forms
that tunnel in vegetable ooze, were of an unhealthy
type. But yet these creatures are as much the
work of God as the flowers and trees, the brisk animals which we love to see about us. We are obliged in self-defence to do battle with the creatures

which menace our health; we do not question our right to deprive them of life for our own comfort; but surely with this analogy before us, we are equally compelled to think of the forms of moral evil, with all their dark vitality, as the work of God's hand.   It is a sad conclusion to be obliged to draw, but I can have no doubt that no comprehensive system of philosophy can ever be framed, which does not trace the vitality of what we call evil to the same hand as the vitality of what we call good.   I have no doubt myself of the supremacy of a single power; but the explanation that evil came into the world by the institution of free-will, and that suffering is the result of sin, seems to me to be wholly inadequate, because the mystery of strife and pain and death is " far older than any history which is written in any book."   The mistake that we make is to count up all the qualities which seem to promote our health and happiness, and to invent an anthropomorphic figure of God, whom we array upon the side which we wish to prevail.   The truth is far darker, far sterner, far more mysterious. The darkness is his not less than the light; selfishness and sin are the work of his hand, as much as unselfishness and holiness.   To call this attitude of mind pessimism, and to say that it can only end in acquiescence or despair, is a sin against truth.   A creed that does not take this thought into account is

nothing but a delusion, with which we try to beguile the seriousness of the truth which we dread;
but such a stern belief does not forbid us to struggle and to strive; it rather bids us believe that effort
is a law of our natures, that we are bound to be en-
listed for the fight, and that the only natures that
fail are those that refuse to take a side at all.

There is no indecision in nature, though there is
some illusion. The very star that rises, pale and
serene, above the darkening thicket, is in reality a
globe wreathed in fiery vapour, the centre of a
throng of whirling planets. What we have to do
is to see as deep as we can into the truth of things,
not to invent paradises of thought, sheltered gardens, from which grief and suffering shall tear us,
naked and protesting; but to gaze into the heart of
God, and then to follow as faithfully as we can the
imperative voice that speaks within the soul.

XXXVII

THERE sometimes falls upon me a great hunger
of heart, a sad desire to build up and renew something—a broken building it may be, a fading flower,
a failing institution, a ruinous character. I feel a
great and vivid pity for a thing which sets out to
be so bright and beautiful, and lapses into shapeless
and uncomely neglect. Sometimes, indeed, it must

be a desolate grief, a fruitless sorrow: as when a flower that has stood on one's table, and cheered the air with its freshness and fragrance, begins to droop, and to grow stained and sordid. Or I see some dying creature, a wounded animal; or even some well-loved friend under the shadow of death, with the hue of health fading, the dear features sharpening for the last change; and then one can only bow, with such resignation as one can muster, before the dreadful law of death, pray that the passage may not be long or dark, and try to dream of the bright secrets that may be waiting on the other side.

But sometimes it is a more fruitful sadness, when one feels that decay can be arrested, that new life can be infused; that a fresh start may be taken, and a life may be beautifully renewed, and be even the brighter, one dares to hope, for a lapse into the dreary ways of bitterness.

This sadness is most apt to beset those who have anything to do with the work of education. One feels sometimes, with a sudden shiver, as when the shadow of a cloud passes over a sunlit garden, that many elements are at work in a small society; that an evil secret is spreading over lives that were peaceful and contented, that suspicion and disunion and misunderstanding are springing up, like poisonous weeds, in the quite corner that God has given one to dress and keep. Then perhaps one tries to put one's hand on what is amiss; sometimes one does too much, and in the wrong way; one has not enough faith, one dares not leave enough to God. Or from timidity or diffidence, or from the base desire not to be troubled, from the poor hope that perhaps things will straighten themselves out, one does too little; and that is the worst shadow of all, the shadow of cowardice or sloth.

Sometimes, too, one has the grief of seeing a slow and subtle change passing over the manner and face of one for whom one cares—not the change of languor or physical weakness; that can be pityingly borne; but one sees innocence withering, indifference to things wholesome and fair creeping on, even sometimes a ripe and evil sort of beauty maturing, such as comes of looking at evil unashamed, and seeing its strong seductiveness. One feels instinctively that the door which had been open before between such a soul and one's own spirit is being slowly and firmly closed, or even, if one attempts to open it, pulled to with a swift motion; and then one may hear sounds within, and even see, in that moment, a rush of gliding forms, that makes one sure that a visitant is there, who has brought with him a wicked company; and then one has to wait in sadness, with now and then a timid knocking, even happy, it may be, if the soul sometimes call fretfully within, to say that it is occupied and cannot come forth.

But sometimes, God be praised, it is the other way. A year ago a man came at his own request to see me. I hardly knew him; but I could see at once that he was in the grip of some hard conflict, which withered his natural bloom. I do not know how all came to be revealed; but in a little while he was speaking with simple frankness and naturalness of all his troubles, and they were many. What was the most touching thing of all was that he spoke as if he were quite alone in his experience, isolated and shut off from his kind, in a peculiar horror of darkness and doubt; as if the thoughts and difficulties at which he stumbled had never strewn a human path before. I said but little to him; and, indeed, there was but little to say. It was enough that he should " cleanse the stuff'd bosom of the perilous stuff that weighs upon the heart." I tried to make him feel that he was not alone in the matter, and that other feet had trodden the dark path before him. No advice is possible in such cases; " therein the patient must minister to himself "; the solution lies in the mind of the sufferer. He knows what he ought to do; the difficulty is for him sufficiently to desire to do it; yet even to speak frankly of cares and troubles is very often to melt and disperse the morbid mist that gathers round them, which grows in solitude. To state them makes them plain and simple; and, indeed, it is more than that; for I have often noticed that the mere act of formulating one's difficulties in the hearing of one who sympathises and feels, often brings the solution with it. One finds, like Christian in Doubting Castle, the key which has lain in one's bosom all the time—the key of Promise; and when one has finished the recital one is lost in bewilderment that one ever was in any doubt at all.

A year has passed since that date, and I have had the happiness of seeing health and contentment stream back into the man's face. He has not overcome, he has not won an easy triumph; but he is in the way now, not wandering on trackless hills.

So, in the mood of which I spoke at first—the mood in which one desires to build up and renew —one must not yield one's self to luxurious and pathetic reveries, or allow one's self to muse and wonder in the half-lit region in which one may beat one's wings in vain—the region, I mean, of sad stupefaction as to why the world is so full of broken dreams, shattered hopes, and unfulfilled possibilities. One must rather look round for some little definite failure that is within the circle of one's vision. And even so, there sometimes comes what is the most evil and subtle temptation of all, which creeps upon the mind in lowly guise, and preaches inaction. What concern have you, says the tempting voice, to meddle with the lives and characters of others—to guide, to direct, to help—when there is so much that is bitterly amiss with your own heart and life? How will you dare to preach what you do not practise? The answer of the brave heart is that, if one is aware of failure, if one has suffered, if one has gathered experience, one must be ready to share. If I falter and stumble under my own heavy load, which I have borne so querulously, so clumsily, shall not I say a word which can help a fellow-sufferer to bear his load more easily, help him to avoid the mistakes, the falls into which my own perversity has betrayed me? To make another's burden lighter is to lighten one's own burden; and, sinful as it may be to err, it is still more sinful to see another err and be silent, to withhold the word that might save him. Perhaps no one can help so much as one that has suffered himself, who knows the turns of the sad road, and the trenches which beset the way.

For thus comes most truly the joy of repentance; it is joy to feel that one's own lesson is learned, and that the feeble feet are a little stronger; but if one may also feel that another has taken heed, has been saved the fall that must have come if he had not been warned, one does not grudge one's own pain, that has brought a blessing with it, that is outside

of one's own blessing; one hardly even grudges the
sin.

XXXVIII

I HAVE been away from my books lately, in a
land of downs and valleys; I have walked much
alone, or with a silent companion—that greatest
of all luxuries. And, as is always the case when
I get out of the reach of books, I feel that I read
a great deal too much, and do not meditate enough.
It sounds indolent advice to say that one ought to
meditate; but I cannot help feeling that reading is
often a still more indolent affair. When I am
alone, or at leisure among my books I take a volume down; and the result is that another man does
my thinking for me. It is like putting one's self in a
comfortable railway carriage; one runs smoothly
along the iron track, one stops at specified stations,
one sees a certain range of country, and an abundance of pretty things in flashes—too many, indeed,
for the mind to digest; and that is the reason, I
think, why a modern journey, even with all the
luxuries that surround it, is so tiring a thing. But
to meditate is to take one's own path among the
hills; one turns off the track to examine anything
that attracts the attention; one makes the most of
the few things that one sees.

Reading is often a mere saving of trouble, a soporific for a restless brain. This last week, as I say, I have had very few books with me. One of the few has been Milton's *Paradise Lost,* and I have read it from end to end. I want to say a few words about the book first, and then to diverge to a larger question. I have read the poem with a certain admiration; it is a large, strong, rugged, violent thing. I have, however, read it without emotion, except that a few of the similes in it, which lie like shells on a beach of sand, have pleased me. Yet it is not true to say that I have read it without emotion, because I have read it with anger and indignation. I have come to the conclusion that the book has done a great deal of harm. It is responsible, I think, for a great many of the harsh, business-like, dismal views of religion that prevail among us. Milton treated God, the Saviour, and the angels, from the point of view of a scholar who had read the *Iliad.* I declare that I think that the passages where God the Father speaks, discusses the situation of affairs, and arranges matters with the Saviour, are some of the most profane and vicious passages in English literature. I do not want to be profane myself, because it is a disgusting fault; but the passage where the scheme of Redemption is arranged, where God enquires whether any of the angels will undergo death in order to satisfy his sense of injured justice, is a passage of what I can only call stupid brutality, disguised, alas, in the solemn and majestic robe of sonorous language. The angels timidly decline, and the Saviour volunteers, which saves the shameful situation. The character of God, as displayed by Milton, is that of a commercial, complacent, irritable Puritan. There is no largeness or graciousness about it, no wistful love. He keeps his purposes to himself, and when his arrangements break down, as indeed they deserve to do, some one has got to be punished. If the guilty ones cannot, so much the worse; an innocent victim will do, but a victim there must be. It is a wicked, an abominable passage, and I would no more allow an intelligent child to read it than I would allow him to read an obscene book.

Then, again, the passage where the rebel angels cast cannon, make gunpowder, and mow the good angels down in rows, is incredibly puerile and ridiculous. The hateful materialism of the whole thing is patent. I wish that the English Church could have an Index, and put *Paradise Lost* upon it, and allow no one to read it until he had reached years of discretion, and then only with a certificate, and for purely literary purposes.

It is a terrible instance how strong a thing Art is; the grim old author, master of every form of ugly vituperation, had drifted miserably away from his beautiful youth, when he wrote the sweet poems and sonnets that make the pedestal for his fame; and on that delicate pedestal stands this hideous iron figure, with its angry gestures, its sickening strength.

I could pile up indignant instances of the further harm the book has done. Who but Milton is responsible for the hard and shameful view of the position of woman? He represents her as a clinging, soft, compliant creature, whose only ideal is to be to make things comfortable for her husband, and to submit to his embraces. Milton spoilt the lives of all the women he had to do with, by making them into slaves, with the same consciousness of rectitude with which he whipped his nephews, the sound of whose cries made his poor girl-wife so miserable. But I do not want to go further into the question of Milton himself. I want to follow out a wider thought which came to me among the downs to-day.

There seems to me to be in art, to take the metaphor of the temple at Jerusalem, three gradations or regions, which may be typified by the Court, the Holy Place, and the Holy of Holies. Into the Court many have admittance, both writers and readers; it is just shut off from the world, but admittance is easy and common. All who are moved and stirred by ideas and images can enter here. Then there is the Holy Place, dark and glorious, where the candlestick glimmers and the altar gleams. And to this place the priests of art have access. Here are to be found all delicate and strenuous craftsmen, all who understand that there are secrets and mysteries in art. They can please and thrill the mind and ear; they can offer up a fragrant incense; but the full mystery is not revealed to them. Here are to be found many graceful and soulless poets, many writers of moving tales, and discriminating critics, who are satisfied, but cannot satisfy. Those who frequent this place are generally of opinion that they know all that is to be known; they talk much of form and colour, of values and order. They can make the most of their materials; and indeed their skill outruns their emotion.

But there is the inmost shrine of all within, where the darkness broods, lit at intervals by the shining of a divine light, that glimmers on the ark and touches the taper wings of the adoring angels. The contents indeed of the sacred chest are of the simplest; a withered branch, a pot of food, two slabs of grey stone, obscurely engraved. Nothing rich or rare. But those who have access to the inner shrine are face to face with the mystery. Some have the skill to hint it, none to describe it. And there are some, too, who have no skill to express themselves, but who have visited the place, and bring back some touch of radiance gushing from their brows.

Milton, in his youth, had looked within the shrine, but he forgot, in the clamorous and sordid world, what he had seen. Only those who have visited the Holiest place know those others who have set foot there, and they cannot err. I cannot define exactly what it is that makes the difference. It cannot be seen in performance; for here I will humbly and sincerely make the avowal that I have been within the veil myself, though I know not when or how. I learned there no perfection of skill, no methods of expression. But ever since, I have looked out for the signs that tell me whether another has set foot there or no. I sometimes see the sign in a book, or a picture; sometimes it comes out in talk; and sometimes I discern it in the glance of an eye, for all the silence of the lips. It is not knowledge, it is not pride that the access confers. Indeed it is often a sweet humility of soul. It is nothing definite; but it is a certain attitude of mind, a certain quality of thought. Some of those who have been within are very sinful persons, very unhappy, very unsatisfactory, as the world would say. But they are never perverse or wilful natures; they are never cold or mean. Those in whom coldness and meanness are found are of necessity excluded from the Presence. But though the power to step behind the veil seldom brings serenity, or strength, or confidence, yet it is the best thing that can happen to a man in the world.

Some perhaps of those who read these words will think that it is all a vain shadow, and that I am but wrapping up an empty thought in veils of words. But though I cannot explain, though I cannot say what the secret is, I can claim to be able to say almost without hesitation whether a human spirit has passed within; and more than that. As I write these words, I know that if any who have set foot in the secret shrine read them, they will understand, and recognise that I am speaking a simple truth.

Some, indeed, find their way thither through religion; but none whose religion is like Milton's. Indeed, part of the wonder of the secret is the infinite number of paths that lead there; they are all lonely; the moment is unexpected; indeed, as was the case with myself, it is possible to set foot within, and yet not to know it at the time.

It is this secret which constitutes the innermost brotherhood of the world. The innermost, I say, because neither creed, nor nationality, nor occupation, nor age, nor sex affects the matter. It is difficult, or shall I say unusual, for the old to enter; and most find the way there in youth, before habit and convention have become tyrannous,

and have fenced the path of life with hedges and
walls.

Again it is the most secret brotherhood of the
world; no one can dare to make public proclama-
tion of it, no one can gather the saints together, for
the essence of the brotherhood is its isolation.   One
may indeed recognise a brother or a sister, and that
is a blessed moment; but one must not speak of it
in words; and indeed there is no need of words,
where all that matters is known.   It may be asked
what are the benefits which this secret brings.   It
does not bring laughter, or prosperity, or success,
or even cheerfulness; but it brings a high, though
fitful, joy—a joy that can be captured, practised,
retained.   No one can, I think, of set purpose, capture the secret.   No one can find the way by desiring it.   And yet the desire to do so is the seed of
hope.   And if it be asked, why I write and print
these veiled words about so deep and intimate a
mystery, I would reply that it is because not all who
have found the way, know that they have found it;
and my hope is that these words of mine may show
some restless hearts that they have found it.   For
one may find the shrine in youth, and for want of
knowing that one has found it, may forget it in
middle age; and that is what I sorrowfully think
that not a few of my brothers do.   And the sign
of such a loss is that such persons speak contempt-

uously and disdainfully of their visions, and try to laugh and deride the young and gracious out of such hopes; which is a sin that is hateful to God, a kind of murder of souls.

And now I have travelled a long way from where I began, but the path was none of my own making. It was Milton, that fierce and childish poet, that held open the door, and within I saw the ladder, at the fiery head of which is God himself. And like Jacob (who was indeed of our company) I made a pillow for my head of the stones of the place, that I might dream more abundantly.

And so, as I walked to-day among the green places of the down, I made a prayer in my heart to God, the matter of which I will now set down; and it was that all of us who have visited that most Holy Place may be true to the vision; and that God may reveal us to each other, as we go on pilgrimage; and that as the world goes forward, he may lead more and more souls to visit it, that bare and secret place, which yet holds more beauty than the richest palace of the world. For palaces but hold the outer beauty in types and glimpses and similitudes. While in secret shrine we visit the central fountain-head, from which the water of life, clear as crystal, breaks in innumerable channels, and flows out from beneath the temple door, as Ezekiel saw it flow, lingering and delaying, but surely coming to glad-

den the earth.   I could indeed go further, and speak
many things out of a full heart about the matter.
I could quote the names of many poets and artists,
great and small; and I could say which of them be-
longs to the inner company, and which of them is
outside.   But I will not do this, because it would
but set inquisitive people puzzling and wondering,
and trying to guess the secret; and that I have no
desire to do; because these words are not written
to make those who do not understand to be curious;
but they are written to those who know, and, most
of all, to those who know but have forgotten.   No
one may traffic in these things; and indeed there is
no opportunity to do so.   I could learn in a moment, from a sentence or a smile, if one had the
secret; and I could spend a long summer day trying to explain it to a learned and intelligent person,
and yet give no hint of what I meant.   For the
thing is not an intelligible process, a matter of rea-
soning and logic; it is an intuition.   And therefore
it is that those who cannot believe in anything that
they do not understand, will think these words of
mine to be folly and vanity.   The only case where
I have found a difficulty in deciding, is when I talk
to one who has lived much with those who had the
secret, and has caught, by a kind of natural imita-
tion, some of the accent and cadence of the truth.
An old friend of mine, a pious woman, used in her

last days to have prayers and hymns read much in her room; there was a parrot that sat there in his cage, very silent and attentive; and not long after, when the parrot was ill, he used to mutter prayers and hymns aloud, with a devotion that would have deceived the very elect. And it is even so with the people of whom I have spoken. Not long ago I had a long conversation with one, a clever woman, who had lived much in the house of a man who had seen the truth; and I was for a little deceived, and thought that she also knew the truth. But suddenly she made a hard judgment of her own, and I knew in a moment that she had never seen the shrine.

And now I have said enough, and must make an end. I remember that long ago, when I was a boy, I painted a picture on a panel, and set it in my room. It was the figure of a kneeling youth on a hillock, looking upwards; and beyond the hillock came a burst of rays from a hidden sun. Underneath it, for no reason that I can well explain, I painted the words φῶς ἐθεασάμην καὶ ἔμφοβος ἦν—*I beheld a light and was afraid.* I was then very far indeed from the sight of the truth; but I know now that I was prophesying of what should be; for the secret sign of the mystery is a fear, not a timid and shrinking fear, but a holy and transfiguring awe. I little guessed what would some day befall me;

but now that I have seen, I can only say with all my heart that it is better to remember and be sad, than to forget and smile.

XXXIX

I WAS awakened this morning, at the old house where I am staying, by low and sweet singing. The soft murmur of an organ was audible, on which some clear trebles seemed to swim and float—one voice of great richness and force seeming to utter the words, and to draw into itself the other voices, appropriating their tone but lending them personality. These were the words I heard—

" The High Priest once a year
Went in the Holy Place
With garments white and clear,
It was the day of Grace.

Without the people stood,
While unseen and alone
With incense and with blood
He did for them atone.

So we without abide
A few short passing years,
While Christ who for us died
Before our God appears.

Before His Father there
His sacrifice He pleads,
And with unceasing prayer
For us He intercedes."

The sweet sounds ceased; the organ lingered for an instant in a low chord of infinite sweetness, and then a voice was heard in prayer. That there was a chapel in the house I knew, and that a brief morning prayer was read there. But I could not help wondering at the remarkable distinctness with which I heard the words—they seemed close to my ear in the air beside me. I got up, and drawing my curtains found that it was day; and then I saw that a tiny window in the corner of my room, that gave on the gallery of the chapel, had been left open, by accident or design, and that thus I had been an auditor of the service.

I found myself pondering over the words of the hymn, which was familiar to me, though strangely enough is to be found in but few collections. It is a perfect lyric, both in its grave language and its beautiful balance; and it is too, so far as such a composition can be, or ought to be, intensely dramatic. The thought is just touched, and stated with exquisite brevity and restraint; there is not a word too much or too little; the image is swiftly presented, the inner meaning flashed upon the mind. It seemed to me, too, a beautiful and desirable thing to begin the day thus, with a delicate hallowing of the hours; to put one gentle thought into the heart, perfumed by the sweet music. But then my reflections took a further drift; beautiful as the lit-

tle ceremony was, noble and refined as the thought
of the tender hymn was, I began to wonder whether
we do well to confine our religious life to so
restricted a range of ideas. It seemed almost ungrateful to entertain the thought, but I felt a certain bewilderment as to whether this remote image,
drawn from the ancient sacrificial ceremony, was
not even too definite a thought to feed the heart
upon. For strip the idea of its fair accessories, its
delicate art, and what have we but the sad belief,
drawn from the dark ages of the world, that the
wrathful Creator of men, full of gloomy indignation at their perverseness and wilfulness, needs the
constant intercession of the Eternal Son, who is
too, in a sense, himself, to appease the anger with
which he regards the sheep of his hand. I cannot
really in the depths of my heart echo that dark belief. I do not indeed know why God permits such
blindness and sinfulness among men, and why he
allows suffering to cloud and darken the world.
But it would cause me to despair of God and man
alike, if I felt that he had flung our pitiful race into
the world, surrounded by temptation both within
and without, and then abandoned himself to anger
at their miserable dalliance with evil. I rather believe that we are rising and struggling to the light,
and that his heart is with us, not against us in the
battle. It may of course be said that all that kind

of Calvinism has disappeared; that no rational
Christians believe it, but hold a larger and a wider
faith. I think that this is true of a few intelligent
Christians, as far as the dropping of Calvinism
goes, though it seems to me that they find it somewhat difficult to define their faith; but as to Calvinism having died out in England, I do not think
that there is any reason to suppose that it has done
so; I believe that a large majority of English
Christians would believe the above-quoted hymn to
be absolutely justified in its statements both by
Scripture and reason, and that a considerable min-
ority would hardly consider it definite enough.

But then came a larger and a wider thought.
We talk and think so carelessly of the divine revelation; we, who have had a religious bringing up, who
have been nurtured upon Israelite chronicles and
prophecies, are inclined, or at least predisposed, to
think that the knowledge of God is written larger
and more directly in these records, the words of
anxious and troubled persons, than in the world
which we see about us. Yet surely in field and
wood, in sea and sky, we have a far nearer and more
instant revelation of God. In these ancient records we have the thoughts of men, intent upon their
own schemes and struggles, and looking for the
message of God, with a fixed belief that the history
of one family of the human race was his special and

particular prepossession. Yet all the while his immediate Will was round them, written in a thousand forms, in bird and beast, in flower and tree. He permits and tolerates life. He deals out joy and sorrow, life and death. Science has at least revealed a far more vast and inscrutable force at work in the world, than the men of ancient days ever dreamed of.

Do we do well to confine our religious life to these ancient conceptions? They have no doubt a certain shadow of truth in them; but while I know for certain that the huge Will of God is indeed at work around me, in every field and wood, in every stream and pool, do I *really* know, do I honestly believe that any such process as the hymn indicates, is going on in some distant region of heaven? The hymn practically pre-supposes that our little planet is the only one in which the work of God is going forward. Science hints to me that probably every star that hangs in the sky has its own ring of planets, and that in every one of these some strange drama of life and death is proceeding. It is a dizzy thought! But if it be true, is it not better to face it? The mind shudders, appalled at the immensity of the prospect. But do not such thoughts as these give us a truer picture of ourselves, and of our own humble place in the vast complexity of things, than the excessive dwelling upon the wistful dreams of ancient law-givers and prophets? Or is it better to delude ourselves? Deliberately to limit our view to the history of a single race, to a few centuries of records? Perhaps that may be a more practical, a more effective view; but when once the larger thought has flashed into the mind, it is useless to try and drown it.

Everything around me seems to cry aloud the warning, not to aim at a conceit of knowledge about these deep secrets, but to wait, to leave the windows of the soul open for any glimpse of truth from without.

To beguile the time I took up a volume near me, the work of a much decried poet, Walt Whitman. Apart from the exquisite power of expression that he possesses, he always seems to me to enter, more than most poets, into the largeness of the world, to keep his heart fixed on the vast wonder and joy of life. I read that poem full of tender pathos and suggestiveness, *A Word out of the Sea,* where the child, with the wind in his hair, listens to the lament of the bird that has lost his mate, and tries to guide her wandering wings back to the deserted nest. While the bird sings, with ever fainter hope, its little heart aching with the pain of loss, the child hears the sea, with its " liquid rims and wet sands " breathing out the low and delicious word *death.*

The poet seems to think of death as the loving

answer to the yearning of all hearts, the sleep that closes the weary eyes. But I cannot rise to this thought, tender and gentle as it is.

If indeed there be another life beyond death, I can well believe that death is in truth an easier and simpler thing than one fears; only a cloud on the hill, a little darkness upon Nature. But God has put it into my heart to dread it; and he hides from me the knowledge of whether indeed there be another side to it. And while I do not even know that, I can but love life, and be fain of the good days. All the religion in the world depends upon the belief that, set free from the bonds of the flesh, the spirit will rest and recollect. But is that more than a hope? Is it more than the passionate instinct of the heart that cannot bear the thought that it may cease to be?

I seem to have travelled far away from the hymn that sounded so sweetly in my ears; but I return to the thought; is not, I will ask, the poet's reverie—the child with his wet hair floating in the sea-breeze, the wailing of the deserted bird, the waves that murmur that death is beautiful—is not this all more truly and deeply religious than the hymn which speaks of things, that not only I cannot affirm to be true, but which, if true, would plunge me into a deeper and cheaper hopelessness even than that in which my ignorance condemns me to live? Ought

we not, in fact, to try and make our religion a much
wider, quieter thing? Are we not exchanging the
melodies of the free birds that sing in the forest
glade, for the melancholy chirping of the caged
linnet? It seems to me often as though we had
captured our religion from a multitude of fair hov-
ering presences, that would speak to us of the
things of God, caged it in a tiny prison, and closed
our ears to the larger and wider voices?

I walked to-day in sheltered wooded valleys; and
at one point, in a very lonely and secluded lane,
leaned long upon a gate that led into a little forest
clearing, to watch the busy and intent life of the
wood. There were the trees extending their fresh
leaves to the rain; the birds slipped from tree to
tree; a mouse frisked about the grassy road; a
hundred flowers raised their bright heads. None
of these little lives have, I suppose, any conception
of the extent of life that lies about them; each of
them knows the secrets and instincts of its own tiny
brain, and guesses perhaps at the thoughts of the
little lives akin to it. Yet every tiniest, shortest,
most insignificant life has its place in the mind of
God. It seemed to me then such an amazing, such
an arrogant thing to define, to describe, to limit the
awful mystery of the Creator and his purpose.
Even to think of him, as he is spoken of in the Old
Testament, with fierce and vindictive schemes, with

flagrant partialities, seemed to me nothing but a dreadful profanation. And yet these old writings do, in a degree, from old association, colour my thoughts about him.

And then all these anxious visions left me; and I felt for awhile like a tiny spray of seaweed floating on an infinite sea, with the brightness of the morning overhead. I felt that I was indeed set where I found myself to be, and that if now my little heart and brain are too small to hold the truth, yet I thanked God for making even the conception of the mystery, the width, the depth, possible to me; and I prayed to him that he would give me as much of the truth as I could bear. And I do not doubt that he gave me that; for I felt for an instant that whatever befall me, I was indeed a part of Himself; not a thing outside and separate; not even his son and his child: but Himself.

XL

I HAD so strange a dream or vision the other night, that I cannot refrain from setting it down; because the strangeness and the wonder of it seem to make it impossible for me to have conceived of it myself; it was suggested by nothing, originated by nothing that I can trace; it merely came to me out of the void.

After confused and troubled dreams of terror and bewilderment, enacted in blind passages and stifling glooms, with crowds of unknown figures passing rapidly to and fro, I seemed to grow suddenly light-hearted and joyful. I next appeared to myself to be sitting or reclining on the grassy top of a cliff, in bright sunlight. The ground fell precipitously in front of me, and I saw to left and right the sharp crags and horns of the rock-face below me; behind me was a wide space of grassy down, with a fresh wind racing over it. The sky was cloudless. Far below I could see yellow sands, on which a blue sea broke in crisp waves. To the left a river flowed through a little hamlet, clustered round a church; I looked down on the roofs of the small houses, and saw people passing to and fro, like ants. The river spread itself out in shallow shining channels over the sand, to join the sea. Further to the left rose shadowy headland after headland, and to the right lay a broad well-watered plain, full of trees and villages, bounded by a range of blue hills. On the sea moved ships, the wind filling their sails, and the sun shining on them with a peculiar brightness. The only sound in my ears was that of the whisper of the wind in the grass and stone crags.

But I soon became aware with a shock of pleasant surprise that my perception of the whole scene was of a different quality to any perception I had before experienced. I have spoken of seeing and hearing: but I became aware that I was doing neither; the perceptions, so to speak, both of seeing and hearing were not distinct, but the same. I was aware, for instance, at the same moment, of the *whole* scene, both of what was behind me and what was in front of me. I have described what I saw successively, because there is no other way of describing it; but it was all present at once in my mind, and I had no need to turn my attention to one point or another, but everything was there before me, in a unity at which I cannot even hint in words. I then became aware too, that, though I have spoken of myself as seated or reclined, I had no body, but was merely, as it were, a sentient point. In a moment I became aware that to transfer that sentience to another point was merely an act of will. I was able to test this; in an instant I was close above the village, which a moment before was far below me, and I perceived the houses, the very faces of the people close at hand; at another moment I was buried deep in the cliff, and felt the rock with its fissures all about me; at another moment, following my wish, I was beneath the sea, and saw the untrodden sands about me, with the blue sunlit water over my head. I saw the fish dart and poise above me, the ribbons of sea-weed floating up, just swayed

by the currents, shells crawling like great snails on
the ooze, crabs hurrying about among piles of
boulders. But something drew me back to my first
station, I know not why; and there I poised, as a
bird might have poised, and lost myself in a blissful
dream. Then it darted into my mind that I was
what I had been accustomed to call dead. So this
was what lay on the other side of the dark passage,
this lightness, this perfect freedom, this undreamed-
of peace! I had not a single care or anxiety. It
seemed as if nothing could trouble my repose and
happiness. I could only think with a deep compassion of those who were still pent in uneasy bodies, under strait and sad conditions, anxious, sad,
troubled, and blind, not knowing that the shadow
of death which encompassed them was but the cloud
which veiled the gate of perfect and unutterable
happiness.

I felt rising in my mind a sense of all that lay
before me, of all the mysteries that I would penetrate, all the unvisited places that I would see. But
at present I was too full of peace and quiet happiness to do anything but stay in an infinite content
where I was. All sense of *ennui* or restlessness had
left me. I was utterly free, utterly blest. I did, indeed, once send my thought to the home which I
loved, and saw a darkened house, and my dear ones
moving about with grief written legibly on their

faces.   I saw my mother sitting looking at some
letters which I perceived to be my own, and was
aware that she wept.   But I could not even bring
myself to grieve at that, because I knew that the
same peace and joy that filled me was also surely
awaiting them, and the darkest passage, the sharpest human suffering, seemed so utterly little and
trifling in the light of my new knowledge; and I
was soon back on my cliff-top again, content to
wait, to rest, to luxuriate in a happiness which
seemed to have nothing selfish about it, because the
satisfaction was so perfectly pure and natural.

While I thus waited I became aware, with the
same sort of sudden perception, of a presence beside me.   It had no outward form; but I knew that
it was a spirit full of love and kindness: it seemed
to me to be old; it was not divine, for it brought no
awe with it; and yet it was not quite human; it was
a spirit that seemed to me to have been human, but
to have risen into a higher sphere of perception.   I
simply felt a sense of deep and pure companion-
ship.   And presently I became aware that some
communication was passing between my consciousness and the consciousness of the newly-arrived
spirit.   It did not take place in words, but in
thought; though only by words can I now represent it.

" Yes," said the other, " you do well to rest and

to be happy: is it not a wonderful experience? and yet you have been through it many times already, and will pass through it many times again."

I suppose that I did not wholly understand this, for I said: "I do not grasp that thought, though I am certain it is true: have I then died before?"

"Yes," said the other, "many times. It is a long progress; you will remember soon, when you have had time to reflect, and when the sweet novelty of the change has become more customary. You have but returned to us again for a little; one needs that, you know, at first; one needs some refreshment and repose after each one of our lives, to be renewed, to be strengthened for what comes after."

All at once I understood. I knew that my last life had been one of many lives lived at all sorts of times and dates, and under various conditions; that at the end of each I had returned to this joyful freedom.

It was the first cloud that passed over my thought. "Must I return again to life?" I said.

"Oh, yes," said the other; "you see that; you will soon return again—but never mind that now; you are here to drink your fill of the beautiful things which you will only remember by glimpses and visions when you are back in the little life again."

And then I had a sudden intuition. I seemed to

be suddenly in a small and ugly street of a dark town. I saw slatternly women run in and out of the houses; I saw smoke-stained grimy children playing in the gutter. Above the poor, ill-kept houses a factory poured its black smoke into the air, and hummed behind its shuttered windows. I knew in a sad flash of thought that I was to be born there, to be brought up as a wailing child, under sad and sordid conditions, to struggle into a life of hard and hopeless labour, in the midst of vice, and poverty, and drunkenness, and hard usage. It filled me for a moment with a sort of nauseous dread, remembering the free and liberal conditions of my last life, the wealth and comfort I had enjoyed.

"No," said the other; for in a moment I was back again, "that is an unworthy thought—it is but for a moment; and you will return to this peace again."

But the sad thought came down upon me like a cloud. "Is there no escape?" I said; and at that, in a moment, the other spirit seemed to chide me, not angrily, but patiently and compassionately. "One suffers," he said, "but one gains experience; one rises," adding more gently: "We do not know why it must be, of course—but it is the Will; and however much one may doubt and suffer in the dark world there, one does not doubt of the wisdom or the love of it here." And I knew in a moment that I did not doubt, but that I would go willingly wherever I should be sent.

And then my thought became concerned with the spirit that spoke with me, and I said, " And what is your place and work? for I think you are like me and yet unlike." And he said: " Yes, it is true; I have to return thither no more; that is finished for me, and I grudge no single step of the dark road: I cannot explain to you what my work or place is; but I am old, and have seen many things; each of us has to return and return, not indeed till we are made perfect, but till we have finished that part of our course; but the blessedness of this peace grows and grows, while it becomes easier to bear what happens in that other place, for we grow strong and simple and sincere, and then the world can hurt us but little. We learn that we must not judge men; but we know that when we see them cruel and vicious and selfish, they are then but children learning their first lessons; and on each of our visits to this place we see that the evil matters less and less, and the hope becomes brighter and brighter; till at last we see." And I then seemed to turn to him in thought, for he said with a grave joy: " Yes, I have seen." And presently I was left alone to my happiness.

How long it lasted I cannot tell; but presently I seemed less free, less light of heart; and soon I knew that I was bound; and after a space I woke into the world again, and took up my burden of cares.

But for all that I have a sense of hopefulness left which I think will not quite desert me. From what dim cell of the brain my vision rose, I know not, but though it came to me in so precise and clear a form, yet I cannot help feeling that something deep and true has been revealed to me, some glimpse of pure heaven and bright air, that lies outside our little fretted lives.

XLI

I HAVE spoken above, I know well, of things in which I have no skill to speak; I know no philosophy or metaphysics; to look into a philosophical book is to me like looking into a room piled up with bricks, the pure materials of thought; they have no meaning for me, until the beautiful mind of some literary architect has built them into a house of life; but just as a shallow pool can reflect the dark and infinite spaces of night, pierced with stars, so in my own shallow mind these perennial difficulties, which lie behind all that we do and say, can be for a moment mirrored.

The only value that such thoughts can have in life is that they should teach us to live in a frank and sincere mood, waiting patiently for the Lord, as the old Psalmist said. My own philosophy is a very simple one, and, if I could only be truer to it, it would bring me the strength which I lack. It is this; that being what we are, such frail, mysterious, inexplicable beings, we should wait humbly and hopefully upon God, not attempting, nor even wishing, to make up our minds upon these deep secrets, only determined that we will be true to the inner light, and that we will not accept any solution which depends for its success upon neglecting or overlooking any of the phenomena with which we are confronted. We find ourselves placed in the world, in definite relations with certain people, endowed with certain qualities, with faults and fears, with hopes and joys, with likes and dislikes. Evil haunts us like a shadow, and though it menaces our happiness, we fall again and again under its dominion; in the depths of our spirit a voice speaks, which assures us again and again that truth and purity and love are the best and dearest things that we can desire; and that voice, however, imperfectly, I try to obey, because it seems the strongest and clearest of all the voices that call to me. I try to regard all experience, whether sweet or bitter, fair or foul, as sent me by the great and awful power that put me where I am. The strongest and best things in the world seem to me to be peace and tranquillity, and the same hidden power seems to be leading me thither; and to lead me all the faster whenever I try not to fret, not to grieve, not to despair. *"Casting all your care upon him, for he careth for you,"* says the Divine Word; and the more that I follow intuition rather than reason, the nearer I seem to come to the truth. I have lately wasted much fruitless thought over an anxious decision, weighing motives, forecasting possibilities. I knew at the time how useless it all was, and that my course would be made clear at the right moment; and I will tell the story of how it was made clear, as testimony to the perfect guidance of the divine hand. I was taking a journey, and the weary process was going on in my mind; every possible argument for and against the step was being reviewed and tested; I could not read, I could not even look abroad upon the world. The train drew up at a dull suburban station, where our tickets were collected. The signal was given, and we started. It was at this moment that the conviction came, and I saw how I must act, with a certainty which I could not gainsay or resist. My reason had anticipated the opposite decision, but I had no longer any doubt or hesitation. The only question was how and when to announce the result; but when I returned home the same evening there was the letter waiting for me which gave the very opportunity I desired; and I have since learnt without surprise that the letter was being penned at the very moment when the conviction came to me.

I have told this experience in detail, because it seems to me to be a very perfect example of the suddenness with which conviction comes. But neither do I grudge the anxious reveries which for many days had preceded that conviction, because through them I learnt something of the inner weakness of my nature. But the true secret of it all is that we ought to live as far as we can in the day, the hour, the minute; to waste no time in anxious forecasting and miserable regrets, but just do what lies before us as faithfully as possible. Gradually, too, one learns that the restricting of what is called religion to certain times of prayer and definite solemnities is the most pitiful of all mistakes; life lived with the intuition that I have indicated is all religion. The most trivial incident has to be interpreted; every word and deed and thought becomes full of a deep significance. One has no longer any anxious sense of duty; one desires no longer either to impress or influence; one aims only at guarding the quality of all one does or says—or rather the very word "aims" is a wrong one; there is no longer any aim or effort, except the effort to feel which way the gentle guiding hand would have us to go; the only sorrow that is possible is when we rather perversely follow our own will and pleasure.

The reason why I desire this book to say its few words to my brothers and sisters of this life, without any intrusion of personality, is that I am so sure of the truth of what I say, that I would not have any one distracted from the principles I have tried to put into words, by being able to compare it with my own weak practice. I am so far from having attained; I have, I know, so many weary leagues to traverse yet, that I would not have my faithless and perverse wanderings known. But the secret waits for all who can throw aside convention and insincerity, who can make the sacrifice with a humble heart, and throw themselves utterly and fearlessly into the hands of God. Societies, organisations, ceremonies, forms, authority, dogma—they are all outside; silently and secretly, in the solitude of one's heart, must the lonely path be found; but the slender track once beneath our feet, all the complicated relations of the world become clear and simple. We have no need to change our path in life, to seek for any human guide, to desire new conditions, because we have the one Guide close to us, closer than friend or brother or lover, and we know that we are set where he would have us to be. Such a belief destroys in a flash all our embarrassment in dealing with others,

all our anxieties in dealing with ourselves. In
dealing with ourselves we shall only desire to be
faithful, fearless, and sincere; in dealing with
others we shall try to be patient, tender, apprecia-
tive, and hopeful. If we have to blame, we shall
blame without bitterness, without the outraged
sense of personal vanity that brings anger with it.
If we can praise, we shall praise with generous
prodigality; we shall not think of ourselves as a
centre of influence, as radiating example and pre-
cept; but we shall know our own failures and difficulties, and shall realise as strongly that others are
led likewise, and that each is the Father's peculiar
care, as we realise it about ourselves. There will
be no thrusting of ourselves to the front, nor an uneasy lingering upon the outskirts of the crowd, because we shall know that our place and our course
are defined. We may crave for happiness, but we
shall not resent sorrow. The dreariest and saddest
day becomes the inevitable, the true setting for our
soul; we must drink the draught, and not fear to
taste its bitterest savour; it is the Father's cup.
That a Christian, in such a mood, can concern himself with what is called the historical basis of the
Gospels, is a thought which can only be met by a
smile; for there stands the record of perhaps the
only life ever lived upon earth that conformed itself, at every moment, in the darkest experiences

that life could bring, entirely and utterly to the Divine Will. One who walks in the light that I have spoken of is as inevitably a Christian as he is a human being, and is as true to the spirit of Christ as he is indifferent to the human accretions that have gathered round the august message.

The possession of such a secret involves no retirement from the world, no breaking of ties, no ecclesiastical exercises, no endeavour to penetrate obscure ideas. It is as simple as the sunlight and the air. It involves no protest, no phrase, no renunciation. Its protest will be an unconcerned example, its phrase will be a perfect sincerity of speech, its renunciation will be what it does, not what it abstains from doing. It will go or stay as the inner voice bids it. It will not attempt the impossible, nor the novel. Very clearly, from hour to hour, the path will be made plain, the weakness fortified, the sin purged away. It will judge no other life, it will seek no goal; it will sometimes strive and cry, it will sometimes rest; it will move as gently and simply in unison with the one supreme will, as the tide moves beneath the moon, piled in the central deep with all its noises, flooding the mud-stained waterway, where the ships ride together, or creeping softly upon the pale sands of some sequestered bay.

XLII

I STOP sometimes on a landing in an old house, where I often stay, to look at a dusky, faded water-colour that hangs upon the wall. I do not think its technical merit is great, but it somehow has the poetical quality. It represents, or seems to represent, a piece of high open ground, down-land or heath, with a few low bushes growing there, sprawling and wind-brushed; a road crosses the fore-ground, and dips over to the plain beyond, a forest tract full of dark woodland, dappled by open spaces. There is a long faint distant line of hills on the hori-zon. The time appears to be just after sunset, when the sky is still full of a pale liquid light, be-fore objects have lost their colour, but are just be-ginning to be tinged with dusk. In the road stands the figure of a man, with his back turned, his hand shading his eyes as he gazes out across the plain. He appears to be a wayfarer, and to be weary but not dispirited. There is a look of serene and sober content about him, how communicated I know not. He would seem to have far to go, but yet to be cer-tainly drawing nearer to his home, which indeed he seems to discern afar off. The picture bears the simple legend, *Until the evening*.

This design seems always to be charged for me with a beautiful and grave meaning. Just so would

I draw near to the end of my pilgrimage, wearied but tranquil, assured of rest and welcome. The freshness and blithe eagerness of the morning are over, the solid hours of sturdy progress are gone, the heat of the day is past, and only the gentle descent among the shadows remains, with cool airs blowing from darkling thickets, laden with woodland scents, and the rich fragrance of rushy dingles. Ere the night falls the wayfarer will push the familiar gate open, and see the lamplit windows of home, with the dark chimneys and gables outlined against the green sky. Those that love him are awaiting him, listening for the footfall to draw near.

Is it not possible to attain this? And yet how often does it seem to be the fate of a human soul to stumble, like one chased and haunted, with dazed and terrified air, and hurried piteous phrase, down the darkening track. Yet one should rather approach God, bearing in careful hands the priceless and precious gift of life, ready to restore it if it be his will. God grant us so to live, in courage and trust, that, when he calls us, we may pass willingly and with a quiet confidence to the gate that opens into tracts unknown!

CONCLUSION

And now I will try if I can in a few words to sum up what the purpose of this little volume has been, these pages torn from my book of life, though I hope that some of my readers may, before now, have discerned it for themselves. The Thread of Gold *has two chief qualities.* It is bright, and it is strong; it gleams with a still and precious light in the darkness, glowing with the reflected radiance of the little lamp that we carry to guide our feet, and adding to the ray some rich tinge from its own goodly heart; and it is strong too; it cannot easily be broken; it leads a man faithfully through the dim passages of the cave in which he wanders, with the dark earth piled above his head.*

The two qualities that we should keep with us in our journey through a world where it seems that so much must be dark, are a certain rich fiery essence, a glowing ardour of spirit, a mind of lofty temper, athirst for all that is noble and beautiful. That first; and to that we must add a certain soberness and sedateness of mood, a smiling tranquillity, a true directness of aim, that should lead us not to form our ideas and opinions too swiftly and too firmly; for then we suffer from an anxious vexation*

15

when experience contradicts hope, when things turn out different from what we had desired and supposed. We should deal with life in a generous and high-hearted mood, giving men credit for lofty aims and noble imaginings, and not be cast down if we do not see these purposes blazing and glowing on the surface of things; we should believe that such great motives are there even if we cannot see them; and then we should sustain our lively expectations with a deep and faithful confidence, assured that we are being tenderly and wisely led, and that the things which the Father shows us by the way, if they bewilder, and disappoint, and even terrify us, have yet some great and wonderful meaning, if we can but interpret them rightly. Nay, that the very delaying of these secrets to draw near to our souls, holds within it a strong and temperate virtue for our spirits.

Neither of these great qualities, ardour and tranquillity, can stand alone; if we aim merely at enthusiasm, the fire grows cold, the world grows dreary, and we lapse into a cynical mood of bitterness, as the mortal flame burns low.

Nor must we aim at mere tranquillity; for so we may fall into a mere placid acquiescence, a selfish inaction; our peace must be heartened by eagerness, our zest calmed by serenity. If we follow the fire alone, we become restless and dissatisfied; if we seek only for peace, we become like the patient beasts of the field.

I would wish, though I grow old and grey-haired, a hundred times a day to ask why things are as they are, and to desire that they were otherwise; and again a hundred times a day I would thank God that they are as they are, and praise him for showing me his will rather than my own. For the secret lies in this; that we must not follow our own impulses, and thus grow pettish and self-willed; neither must we float feebly upon the will of God, like a branch that spins in an eddy; rather we must try to put our utmost energy in line with the will of God, hasten with all our might where he calls us, and turn our back as resolutely as we can when he bids us go no further; as an eager dog will intently await his master's choice, as to which of two paths he may desire to take; but the way once indicated, he springs forward, elate and glad, rejoicing with all his might.

He leads me, He leads me; but He has also given me this wild and restless heart, these untamed desires; not that I may follow them and obey them, but that I may patiently discern His will, and do it to the uttermost.

Father, be patient with me, for I yield myself to Thee; Thou hast given me a desirous heart, and

I have a thousand times gone astray after vain shadows, and found no abiding joy. I have been weary many times, and sad often; and I have been light of heart and very glad; but my sadness and my weariness, my lightness and my joy have only blessed me, whenever I have shared them with Thee. I have shut myself up in a perverse loneliness, I have closed the door of my heart, miserable that I am, even upon Thee. And Thou hast waited smiling, till I knew that I had no joy apart from Thee. Only uphold me, only enfold me in Thy arms, and I shall be safe; for I know that nothing can divide us, except my own wilful heart; we forget and are forgotten, but Thou alone rememberest; and if I forget Thee, at least I know that Thou forgettest not me.